A Man Known for Pushing Back

Clint could count four of them. Well . . . three, since he doubted the first one would be getting back up anytime soon. The remaining men spread out and watched him with the eyes of experienced fighters. They gauged his movements and didn't try any hasty attacks of their own.

"We can all walk away from this," Clint said. "After all, I've never seen you boys before in my life."

From what he could see, Clint was every bit the surprise he'd hoped to be. James Halliwell, however, seemed more surprised than all of them combined.

"Leave him out of this," James shouted as the other three men began circling Clint. "Your fight's with me. Let's keep it that way."

The Gunsmith had been hoping things wouldn't go this way—but he didn't have much of a choice anymore. Especially since one of the hired hands was stepping in to take a swing at him with a knife . . .

THE GUNSMITH

253

TANGLED WEB

J. R. ROBERTS

JOVE BOOKS, NEW YORK

This is a work of fiction. Names, characters, places, and incidents either are the product of the author's imagination or are used fictitiously, and any resemblance to actual persons, living or dead, business establishments, events, or locales is entirely coincidental.

TANGLED WEB

A Jove Book / published by arrangement with the author

PRINTING HISTORY
Jove edition / January 2003

Visit our website at
www.penguinputnam.com

ISBN: 0-515-13443-0

A JOVE BOOK®
Jove Books are published by The Berkley Publishing Group,
a division of Penguin Putnam Inc.,
375 Hudson Street, New York, New York 10014.
JOVE and the "J" design
are trademarks belonging to Penguin Putnam Inc.

PRINTED IN THE UNITED STATES OF AMERICA

10 9 8 7 6 5 4 3 2 1

ONE

The sounds of crackling ice drifted through the air all around Clint's head. It sounded as though the ground beneath Eclipse's hooves was about to open up and swallow both horse and rider whole. The Darley Arabian stallion must have been thinking the same thing, and he started nervously shifting from one foot to another.

"Easy, boy," Clint said as he reached out and patted the stallion on its neck. "Shouldn't be much longer now."

Even as he said those words, Clint wondered just how true they could be. As more of a way to pass a few more seconds, he reached into the inner pocket of his jacket and pulled out the folded letter he'd gotten only two days ago.

The message had asked him to be at this spot at this time and didn't say much of anything else. Although he wouldn't normally even think about responding to something blindly like this, Clint recognized the name at the bottom of the note. In fact, he'd even been hoping to meet up with Elena Halliwell during his visit to Barryville, West Virginia.

At first, Clint was surprised to have a letter waiting for him at the front desk of the Hilltop Lodge when he'd checked in. But as soon as he saw the woman's name at

1

the bottom of the neatly folded paper, Clint's surprise
quickly melted away.

The last time he'd been through these parts, he and
Elena had spent quite a bit of time at the Hilltop. The fact
that she knew he'd be showing up in town at this particular time was something else, however. He didn't send
advance word to anyone before arriving in Barryville
since he didn't even decide on going there again until his
travels had brought him within a day's ride of the place.

Elena had been a smart woman, but she wasn't a
fortune-teller. She also didn't seem like the type to get
herself in the kind of situation that would require her to
send for him in such a roundabout way that had to have
been twice as much trouble as coming to pay him a visit
in person.

Clint put his questions in order inside his head as he
folded up the letter and slid it back into his pocket. If
Elena was in trouble, he didn't have any qualms about
helping her out. And if she was trying to put something
over on him by getting him alone all the way out from
the town's borders, then Clint figured it was just as well
for her to do it now and get it over with. After a long
day's ride, Clint was about ready to get a good meal in
his belly and a soft bed beneath the rest of him.

Turning his attention to his surroundings, Clint gave
himself a moment to look around and soak up the atmo-
sphere. With winter on its way out and spring beginning
to stretch its legs and poke its head up, the chill in the air
was blunted by a warmer breeze, which felt cool against
the skin, while giving the snow on the ground a slushy
texture.

White was still the land's predominant color, but it
wasn't covering the trees the way it had been for the previous months. Dark brown wood stuck up from the frost
along with the occasional stubborn bush. The place that
Elena had mentioned in the letter was a spot less than a

mile and a half down the stream that fed into the town's mill.

As Clint sat and watched, he could see chunks of the ice breaking free on the water's surface and trembling slightly in place. Soon, he knew that ice would all be flowing downstream while melting away or breaking into even smaller pieces. And filling the air all around him was the constant cracking of ice as the river thawed out and one frozen chunk ground up against another.

Along with that was another sound. Clint picked it out from all the others in an instant and recognized it immediately as an approaching horse. The animal's hooves broke through the ice-covered snow with a crackle and crunch, drawing nearer at a leisurely pace.

Shifting in his saddle, Clint looked over his shoulder at the other rider. The dark gray horse was easy enough to spot against the background of white. And though he could see the woman's figure sitting on top of the animal, he couldn't make out her features through the layers of coats and scarves.

As if sensing Clint's eyes on her, the rider reached up and pulled down the thin wool scarf that had been wrapped loosely around her face. Her skin was light from spending much of the cold season indoors, but that only made her lips look all the more red and full. Fixing dark brown eyes on Clint, she shook free a thick mane of coppery hair while bringing her horse up alongside Eclipse.

"Good to see you, Elena," Clint said with an approving nod. "You're looking good."

"I'd say the same thing to you, but 'good' just wouldn't do justice to how it feels to see you right now."

TWO

"I wasn't sure you would come," Elena said.

Clint smirked. "That's funny. It seemed to me as though you knew I would be in town even before I did. You knew where I would go for a room and that I'd get your letter. If I think about it hard enough, I'd bet you could tell me what color I'm thinking of right now."

Smiling in the exact way Clint remembered, Elena looked into Clint's eyes and reached out to touch his cheek. She was a small woman, standing less than five and a half feet tall. Even on horseback, she seemed petite and had to lean forward quite a ways to cover the distance separating herself and Clint.

But when her hand made contact with Clint's face, the heat from her skin could be felt through the thin leather gloves she wore. The heat shone in her eyes as well, reminding Clint of the times they'd spent together and all the times they'd looked at each other in the darkness.

"We might not have spent a whole lot of time together, Clint," she said, "but I saw enough to know that you're a creature of habit. You like steak and potatoes for dinner and long nights by a roaring fire for dessert."

"I guess I'll admit to that much."

4

"As for the Hilltop . . . I may sound a little full of myself, but I thought that after the times we had there, you might head there for a room before any of the other hotels in town."

"You got me again. But how did you know I'd be coming here at all? I don't exactly advertise my whereabouts with the local newspapers."

"No, but those papers did catch wind of that business you had in Pennsylvania not too long ago."

"Really?" Clint asked with no small amount of surprise in his voice. Although there had been a tussle there not too long ago, Clint didn't figure it was anything that would make headlines.

"These are quiet parts around here," Elena said by way of explanation. "And the editor of the town's paper used to write dime novels in New York City. I think he still gets a kick out of covering the more colorful stories . . . even if they come from another state."

Nodding, Clint said, "Fine. You knew I was in the area. But that still doesn't explain how you knew I'd be *here*."

Elena's smile took on a somewhat guilty hue and she turned her face in a way that made her look mischievous and seductive at the same time. "I hoped you'd stop by if you were in the area. That letter's been sitting at the front desk of that hotel for over a month now. I was beginning to think you'd forgotten about me, but the more I thought about those nights we spent in that room . . . the more I felt certain that you could never forget. As for you coming back to Barryville . . . blame that on woman's intuition."

Clint wasn't a suspicious man by nature. But living a life filled with men out to fill him full of lead just for the right to brag about it to their friends, Clint had taken to being suspicious as a matter of survival. It wasn't something that ruled his life or made him twitch at every shadow that crossed his path. It was more of a feeling he got in the pit of his stomach that warned him to be on his toes.

He'd gotten that feeling when he'd first read Elena's letter. But the more he looked into her eyes and listened to what she had to say, the more that feeling started to fade away.

After letting another couple of seconds drift by with nothing but the cracking of the ice to fill them, Clint allowed his own smile to show through as he reached out to put his hand on top of hers. "Sorry about all the questions," he said. "But it never hurts to be too careful."

Elena let out a relieved breath and covered Clint's hand. "I didn't mean to make you nervous, but I really needed to talk to you."

"Why didn't you just meet me in town? I would've been along to see you before too long."

"I know. But what I have to say is something I'd rather not say in the open. Especially with someone like . . ." She stopped herself there, glancing up at Clint as though she was uncertain of what words she wanted to use.

Sensing the woman's unease, Clint picked up where she left off. "You mean especially with someone who winds up in the newspaper in at least two different states?"

Elena laughed under her breath. The blush on her cheeks might have come from the nip in the air or the things she was thinking. "I guess that might be it. Well . . . that's exactly it."

"So you found me and picked your spot. Go ahead and say what you wanted to say." When he saw that she wasn't too anxious to speak her mind, Clint picked up on a deeper discomfort that ran just beneath the woman's surface the way the waters of a river flowed beneath the ice. Lowering his voice even though there wasn't another soul to be seen, Clint asked, "Are you in some kind of trouble?"

"It's not me," Elena replied after a short hesitation. "It's James. My brother."

Clint thought for a moment and was unable to recollect any previous mention of Elena even having a brother. Of course, considering the way they'd spent their time the last time he was in town, that wasn't all that surprising.

"Older or younger?" Clint asked.

"What?"

"Your brother. Is he older or younger than you?"

"Oh, he's older. But only by a year and a half."

"And is he the type to get into trouble every so often?"

Elena shook her head. "I know what you must be thinking, Clint. But James isn't the type of man who gets himself into fixes and then needs someone to come and fish him out. Usually, he's the one who's always been there to help out anyone in my family. Most of the town knows they can come to James if they need someone to help them out of a jam."

"He sounds like an upstanding man."

"He is." Her voice was steady as a rock. The caring she felt for him was evident by her tone. "He truly is."

As much as he hated to admit it, that uneasy, suspicious feeling was creeping back into Clint's gut. "So what does a man like that do that makes his sister go behind his back to ask for help from someone like me?"

"James has been looking to make some more money for our family. There's not many of us. Besides James and me, there's just my mother and baby brother. We've got a nice spread outside of town and my mother owns the general store.

"Ever since my father died, things haven't been going so good. We make enough money to live, but James made a promise to my father that he would give us more than what we had. And he's been knocking himself out trying to make good on that."

"He really does sound like a good man," Clint said earnestly.

"That may be his problem."

"How so?"

Elena needed to take a deep breath before continuing. When she'd gathered up enough strength, she said, "My father took over a business from Kyle Bagley some time before he died."

Clint mulled that name over a few times in his head. "Bagley. Bagley . . . he's that land baron who works down around Fort Worth, isn't he?"

"That's right. You know him?"

"I've heard of him. Men as rich as he is tend to be the subject of a lot of conversations. Especially when you get closer to Texas."

"Well, my father acquired the deed to a ranch over in Nebraska and James means to run its herd down to Texas."

"Nebraska's a long way from here."

"James was set to go out on his own with a couple other men to drive the cattle and get things set up over there. When that was done, he figures we'll decide if we want to sell the ranch or move out there to run it full-time."

"You know I'm not much of a rancher, right?" Clint asked, trying not to sound impatient.

Elena nodded. "There's some men who figure they should be the ones to take over that ranch." Lifting her eyes to meet Clint's, she added, "And they're willing to kill him to get their hands on it."

THREE

Having spent his entire life in and around Barryville, James Halliwell was known by the locals there almost as well as they knew their own family members. The man with the bushy beard and stocky build waved to everyone he saw as he made his way from store to store, gathering supplies and food. Whenever his hands got too full, he dumped what he had in the back of a battered old wagon, which was hitched up to a battered old horse.

The routine was the same every two weeks. All of James's family knew where he would be when he went into town.

All of his friends knew.

And even the pair of figures lurking in front of the livery stable knew just where to look if they wanted to find the other man.

If James noticed the two figures watching him as he crossed the street, he gave no indication. The expression on his face remained calm and friendly. His voice never lost its easy tone as he gave and returned greetings from everyone he passed. But even though he went about his affairs as though he didn't have a care in the world, James was being tracked like the only mouse in sight by the two

9

hawks, who stood their ground in front of the stable.

"Howdy, Marna," James said with a nod as he stepped up to the back of his wagon and dropped a sack of grain and some new axe handles into the back.

Marna was an old woman who worked at the bakery. The front of her dress was covered with flour and sugar, which formed a fragrant cloud around her as she stepped onto her porch and batted the white off of herself. Looking up, she smiled warmly and waved. "Hello there, Jimmy. In for supplies?"

"Yes, ma'am."

"Well, you be sure to stop in here and pay me a visit. There'll be some fresh cake in it for you."

"Did you make the sweet frost?"

"Sure did."

"Then I'll see you before you know it."

Once she'd gotten as much of the white powder off of her as she could, Marna gave James one more wave and went back into her bakery. Even in the short time she had the door open to walk inside, the smells of bread and cookies drifted out to tempt the noses of anyone close enough to draw a breath.

James placed everything where he normally did, making sure the heavier sacks were along the edge of the wagon, while the smaller items filled the space in between. In his mind, he was planning out where he needed to go next, even though his path wasn't about to differ from any of the other times he'd bought his supplies.

As soon as he was ready, he turned away from his wagon and started walking toward the general store to finish up his spending for the day. When he was almost there, James glanced over to where the two men had been standing.

Unlike all the other times when he'd noticed the pair from the corner of his eye, the men were no longer perched in their spots. Although James might not have let

on, he'd picked out the two men even before he'd reined
his horse to a stop and jumped down from the wagon's
driver seat. Just as everyone in town knew him inside and
out, James also knew the town in much the same way.

Certain people were always standing in certain spots.
Familiar faces were never too far from where he'd left
them the last time he'd been there, which made two men
such as those relatively easy to spot. That pair had been
eyeballing James all afternoon, but the time he felt most
uncomfortable was when they were no longer there.

All of this ran through his head in the short time it took
for James to step off the street and up onto the boardwalk.
He made sure to keep the same easygoing expression on
his face as he reached out for the door handle and began
to walk inside.

"Tell me somethin', Jimmy," came a voice from just
around the corner. "Ain't shopping and gathering cakes
and such a job for a woman?"

James stopped in his tracks and turned toward the edge
of the building.

Stepping into view, both of the men who had been
watching him from the livery walked around the edge of
the general store and climbed onto the boardwalk. Neither
one of them had James's height or muscular build, but
they still carried themselves as though they were looking
down on him. Their dark clothes were similar to the ones
worn by the rest of the locals, but with one obvious dif-
ference: Neither of the two appeared to have been sullied
by a day's hard work in their lives.

One of them wore the jeans, cotton shirt and leather
jacket of a cowboy while the other was clad in something
a little more formal—his slender frame was covered in a
dark brown suit and matching coat, which came down to
just past his knees.

Both men wore holsters strapped around their waists.
The man in the suit placed his hands on his hips, opening

the coat just enough to reveal another gun holstered beneath his left arm.

"What do you want, Frye?" James asked, trying not to let any emotion whatsoever slip into his voice.

The man in the coat merely smirked. Rather than say anything, he let the other man step forward and speak his own piece.

"I was the one who asked you the question," the man who was dressed like a cowboy said. "Or are you goin' deaf on top of everything else that's wrong with you?"

The only part of James that moved was his eyes. He peeled his gaze away from the man in the coat in such a way that made it seem as though he was nearly about to break something in the process. And when he finally did set his sights on the man in the jacket and jeans, James let his eyes settle in on their new target for a good couple of seconds before speaking.

"If I was you," James said, "I'd leave well enough alone and back the hell away from me right about now."

Instinctively, the man who'd been trying to provoke James Halliwell gnashed his teeth and started to lunge forward. He was stopped by a casual hand slapped across his chest, which affected him the way a short leash affected a dog.

"Maybe you should mind the man," Ezekiel Frye stated. The slender, better dressed of the two kept his focus on James as an amused smile played across his features. "After all . . . you wouldn't want to provoke him while he goes about his shopping and such."

The man in the cowboy gear went by the name of Michael Roth. His wiry body was only slightly bulkier than Frye's, but contained a considerable amount of muscle. The fingers of his right hand brushed over the handle of the .45 revolver hanging at his waist as the muscles in his arm tensed with anticipation. "Is that so?" he asked the man beside him without taking his eyes off of James.

"And why should I worry about provoking a piece of chickenshit like him?"

When Frye smiled a little wider the grimace caused the edges of his waxed mustache to hook upward as though they were each attached to a different fishing line. "Because he just might get upset and start crying or fussing like the prissy little bitch he is."

Hearing that amused Roth to no end. In fact, it seemed to take away his anger for the moment as his body began to shake with building laughter. "That's a good point, Zeke. I never thought of that."

James had to close his eyes for a second and start counting backward from ten to one just the way his sister and mother had suggested. He knew that if he fought the men then and there, he would only be doing exactly what they wanted him to do. Even so, the only thing he could think about besides taking those breaths and counting through those numbers was making both men eat their words.

FOUR

"Who would want to kill your brother?" Clint asked Elena. "Is that ranch worth all that trouble?"

Both she and Clint had climbed down out of their saddles and were walking slowly along the bank of the thawing river. The scenery there was almost soothing enough to take her mind off of everything that had been bothering her recently.

Almost, but not quite.

"The man's name is Ezekiel Frye," she said. "He has interests in nearly every business in town. Most of the men who are on his payroll are nothing but hired guns or crooks. He barely passes for much more than that, himself. But Frye fancies himself as some kind of businessman and forces his way into anything that looks like it might turn any kind of profit."

Clint nodded. He'd come across plenty of men who met that description in his time. Although some of them were more dangerous than others, every single one of them were most definitely trouble. Another constant that he'd discovered when dealing with those types was that they did what they did because they were looking for the quickest road to success. That last part was what didn't settle when Clint thought about the men Elena was describing.

"So what exactly does this Frye want from your brother?" Clint asked.

"He expects James to turn over control of the ranch to his company and step back."

"Just step back and that's it? He didn't even offer to buy him out?"

"He did, but he wasn't even offering half of what the ranch was worth. James figures that driving this herd alone will be worth almost triple what Frye was offering."

"So he told Frye what he could do with his offer."

Elena smiled and nodded. "It sounds like you've met my brother."

"Nah. That's just what I would have done in his place. So what happened after that?"

Elena's smile disappeared quicker than a shadow exposed to the sun. "At first . . . nothing. But then one day I woke up and saw the shed behind our house was on fire. We barely got it out before it would spread and kill someone. One of Frye's men was there watching us as my family and I tried put it out. He didn't do a damn thing. Just stood there and watched."

Elena stopped walking and crossed her arms over her chest. When she spoke, she did so through tightly clenched teeth. Her words came out like steam through a piston. "Later that same day, we got a message from Frye, himself. He gave his offer to buy James out one more time and told him that if he didn't take it that maybe the house would burn next . . . or maybe one of us."

"James went crazy and stormed down to Frye's place in town. I thought he was going to kill him right there in that office of his on Jasper Street, but I knew better than to try and stop him." Looking down at her feet, Elena let out a weak sigh. "I think part of me was hoping he would do something like that when he got there."

Clint let the woman have a few moments to herself before he reached out and put a hand on her shoulder. "Can't say as I blame you for wanting that. Especially after what happened."

She looked at him with a silent thank-you in her eyes and found the strength to straighten herself up and go on. "Of course James did no such thing. In fact, he made it halfway to Frye's office before some of those gun hands I told you about pulled him into an alley and beat the living tar out of him. When James came home, I first thought he wasn't going to make it through the night. Then . . . I thought that he wouldn't rest until Frye was dead for what he done."

Glancing around where she was standing, Elena spotted a fallen log a couple paces away and went over to it. After gathering her skirts about herself, she took a seat on the makeshift bench and folded her hands upon her knees. "James isn't a violent man, Clint. You've got to understand that. But he is proud. Ever since my father died, he's taken it all upon himself to keep the family going and give us all a better life."

"There's plenty of other businesses for him to get in to," Clint said. "If his life is in danger over a ranch that he hasn't even seen yet, then maybe he should just take Frye's offer and let the trouble pass."

Shaking her head, Elena replied, "James would never do that. Not after the fire. Ever since that day, he's been dead-set against giving Frye so much as an inch."

Despite what Clint had just suggested, he couldn't blame Elena's brother one bit for what he was doing. If it had been himself in that same position, he would have rather gone out to Nebraska to run that ranch into the ground himself rather than let someone like Frye get the satisfaction of taking it from him.

"It doesn't matter how many men Frye owns," Elena continued. "James will never back down. I've known him my entire life and I can tell you that much for sure. He won't budge an inch, not even if it . . ." The tears that welled up in her eyes prevented Elena from finishing what she was going to say.

When he saw that, Clint reached out to brush her tears away and finished the sentence she'd started. "Not even if it kills him."

Elena looked as though she might be about to cry in earnest, but only for a moment. Once the tears she'd already shed were wiped from her cheek, she steeled herself and said, "That's right. Even if it kills him. There's no talking to him. Believe me, I've tried more times than I can count and he won't have any of it. He's set on going to that ranch and making it successful just so he can rub it in Frye's face."

"I suppose he wouldn't take any help from the law, either."

"You suppose right. James says this is a family matter and he can handle it on his own." Shrugging, Elena added, "Besides, there's not much Sheriff Williams can do that would be much help. I already asked about that too.

"What it all boils down to is that my family really does need that ranch to pan out. Since my father died, even with James doing his best to support us, we're still only making half of what we did before. It won't be long before we start losing our livestock and land. Soon, Mother's interest in the store will dry up and the house will be the last to go."

"That all sounds terrible," Clint said. "But I still don't see what you want me to do. I know some folks in Nebraska, but not any ranchers or businessmen. There's even fewer people I know out here."

After taking another deep breath, Elena shook off all traces that she'd been crying. Her voice was steady once again and she got to her feet without accepting the helping hand Clint offered. "If James is going to make this trip, I

know that Frye will see to it that he doesn't come back
alive. I need someone to go with him who can help him
safely make the trip there and back again. I don't have
enough money to hire anyone who's good enough in a
fight to do him any good, and James might not let him
come along even if I could."

"I'm not exactly a gun for hire, Elena."

"I know that. But you help out when you can. That's
all I'm asking, Clint. My brother's a good man. Help
him."

Even before Elena had finished talking, Clint had already made up his mind. "Where can I find him?" he
asked.

FIVE

The fact that Frye and Roth were both experienced gun hands was only an afterthought in James's mind. For the time being, the only thing he could see was the smirks on their faces instead of the guns in their holsters.

Frye picked up on this immediately, his nostrils flaring as though he could smell the fury building up inside James's gut. "Hey, Mike," he said to the man beside him. "It looks like I might be wrong about that. Maybe this one here don't belong in a dress after all."

Mike Roth moved as though he was about to take a step forward, but pulled back at the last moment. He tested the air by pulling it in through his nose and letting it out like it was cigarette smoke. "Hell, I seen plenty of women who could get themselves all riled up like that. It don't mean a damn thing."

Despite the fact that he'd heard these insults coming out of those same mouths for some time now, that didn't make it any easier for James to bear. He stored the words in the back of his mind right along with all the others that had been coming ever since the day Zeke Frye had decided to make his life hell on earth. Although it didn't do

19

much to soothe his spirit, it did help to take the edge off
his temper—at least, for the time being.

Any man who made a living from preying on others
had to be a good observer of people. Any predator had to
be able to read their targets to know when they were about
to run or when they were about to crack. Frye watched
every move that James made the way he might watch
actors performing a play. He could tell when James was
getting close to explode and also saw when he managed
to cut the fuse before it burned all the way down.

Putting a hand on Roth's shoulder to pull him back,
Frye stepped forward and kept his watchful eyes fixed on
his target. "You know what your problem is, Jimmy?"

James hated to be called that by these men. What dug
at him even more was that he was certain that Frye knew
how much it got to him, which was why he kept calling
him that whenever the opportunity presented itself.

"I'm not the one with the problem," James said in the
calmest voice he could manage.

Lifting his finger as though he was scolding a child,
Frye winced and shook his head. "That's not exactly true.
You're a solid enough man, but you've got no head for
business. And what's worse than that is that you're
proud."

"A proud man don't do no woman's work," Roth
sneered.

Frye still didn't take his eyes off of James when he
spoke to the man beside him. "Shut up, Mike." The words
were the verbal equivalent of a hand swatting a fly and
Roth took them as such. Although the gunman didn't
seem pleased to be put down in such a way, he wasn't
about to say anything about it, either.

Once he was certain that Roth was going to stay in the
place he'd put him, Frye went on with what he was saying
to James. "Pride doesn't necessarily have to be a bad

thing, Jimmy. But as the Good Book says, that is what cometh before the fall."

James's eyes narrowed and he clenched his fists. "Don't you dare quote scripture to me, you piece of filth. If you had any fear of God in you, you wouldn't be so anxious to hurt me or my family."

"I'm just doing what I have to do to keep my business afloat," Frye replied. He spread his hands in front of him and put on an innocent expression that might have been funny if not for the darkness lurking behind his eyes. "I've made you plenty of offers and you refused every one of them. What else am I supposed to do when dealing with someone who insists on being so unreasonable?"

"I've been asking myself the same thing."

Nodding, Frye said, "Touché. But that still leaves me right where I started." He paused for a second, clasped his hands together and gave James a stare that seemed to drill straight through the back of his skull. "So what would you propose I do to rectify this situation?"

Since he'd had this conversation in one form or another more times than he could rightly count, James took the next couple of moments to look around and get a fix on his own situation. Aside from Roth and Frye, he couldn't spot any of the other men who were on Frye's payroll. He wasn't dumb enough to think that they weren't there, but he was also familiar enough with the businessman to know that he preferred intimidation rather than laying in ambush.

James had been attacked several time by Frye and his men and every one of those times, he'd seen them coming. He couldn't do a damn thing to avoid them, but he'd still seen them coming. That didn't make the beatings and threats easier to bear, but it did give him a good idea on where he stood.

"You want to know what I think you should do about it?" James asked. "I think you should take your threats and all your lies and shove them straight up your ass."

Frye didn't so much as flinch. There wasn't even a muscle in his face that twitched when he heard James speak those words to him. Roth, on the other hand, had enough of a reaction for both himself and his boss.

"Oh, will you look at this," Roth snarled. "It seems this hen thinks he's a rooster, now." His hand dropped down to the gun at his side and his fingers wrapped around the handle. "What do you say now, Zeke? Should he get away with that?"

Frye stood motionless for the span of another couple of breaths. Then, breaking his stony facade with a slow blink, he shrugged and said, "If this is the way he wants to play it, then so be it. Don't say I didn't warn you, Jimmy. And when you're begging for me to stop as your world comes crashing down around you, don't forget that you brought all of this upon yourself."

Just as Roth started to lunge forward, Frye held out his hand to stop the man in his tracks.

"And you know what the unfortunate part of all of this is?" Frye asked. "It's that you brought this all upon your family as well."

And like a master letting go of his hound's leash, Frye pulled his arm back so that Roth could storm forward, wearing a bloodthirsty smile upon his face.

SIX

James didn't think about all the other times he'd locked horns with Frye's men and come out on the losing end. He didn't think about how the boss only hired men who were just as good with their fists as they were with the iron while he was just an angry man with callused knuckles.

He didn't think about these things as Roth came toward him because if he did, he might have lost the courage to stand his ground and jump headfirst into a fight he probably couldn't win. For the moment, the only thing he could think about was the face of his father when he'd been on his deathbed. It was at that moment that James took on the responsibility for providing for his entire family. And that responsibility was what kept him from letting Frye roll over him just so the powerful man would leave him alone.

James's stomach tightened into a fiery knot. His fists clenched so tightly that he could feel his nails digging into his palms. And though every part of him wanted to step back, he forced himself to move forward.

Judging by the look in Roth's eyes, he was more than happy that he wasn't going to be forced to chase James down. Inside his smirk, there was anxiousness and excitement, tempered with just the faintest trace of respect.

"You're gonna take yer beating like a man, huh?" Roth said as he stepped up and started circling his prey like a vulture on two feet. "There might be some guts inside of that carcass of yours after all. How about I tear you open and take a look for myself?"

James couldn't hear what the other man was saying over the rush of blood through his ears. His eyes were too busy searching for a sign of where the first punch was coming from and his ears were too filled with the sounds of his racing heart.

Snapping his head forward in a quick fake, Roth smirked a little more when he saw James swallow up the bait by turning his hands to guard in that direction. He kept one hand firmly on top of his gun while flicking out his other fist, taking full advantage of the opening he'd created. When he felt the jab land in James's stomach, Roth straightened up and started to bounce lightly on the balls of his feet.

"I don't know about them guts," Roth taunted. "They might just be shit and vinegar, after all."

Seeing the other man's confident smile was more than James could bear. Before he knew what he was doing, his own fist was swinging outward in a wide arc aimed for Roth's chin. The other man sidestepped the blow easily before coming in for a second shot.

Roth made a faking maneuver similar to what he'd done the first time, except now he backed it up with a solid punch thrown in that same direction. But James's instincts were still too high-strung for him to cut them off before moving to block a second time.

Luckily, those high-strung reflexes were enough to get James's arms in front of him just quick enough to block the harder blow. Although the impact landed on the bones of his forearms and sent a jolt of pain running up past his elbows, most of the impact was absorbed.

James felt a momentary rush from his block, but wasn't dumb enough to think that the rest of this fight would end so easily. So rather than celebrate his small victory, James put himself on the offensive and shot his left fist in an upward hook directed toward Roth's open midsection.

If James was surprised that he blocked the last punch, he was even more shocked to feel his fist bury itself in his opponent's stomach. The impact felt rich and satisfying after having to listen to Roth's jibes, and the sound of the other man's breath rushing from his lungs was a symphony to James's ears.

Spitting out a curse on the tail end of his hurried exhale, Roth pulled his right hand up and drew the pistol from its holster. From there, he did the first thing he could think of and sent the gun's handle straight into James's face, cracking the polished wood onto the bridge of the other man's nose.

Roth allowed himself a quick smirk, which was instantly wiped off his face by a wild swing from James. The unarmed man's punch clipped Roth squarely on the temple, sending a cascade of bright, flashing blobs swirling behind his eyes.

The punch didn't hurt Roth as much as it caught him off guard. When he tried to move in closer to James, he felt the ground tilt crazily beneath his feet and everything else around him turn in a wobbly circle. Even as the pain started to hit him, it was eclipsed by the rage that boiled up from inside the gunman's depths and only served to fuel his already roaring fire.

"Son of a bitch!" Roth snarled as his vision clouded over into a red haze.

James knew that look only too well since he'd been the one to feel such burning frustration and anger so much over the last couple months. But this was the first time he'd seen that look on Roth. It was also the first time he was thoroughly convinced that he was about to die.

Acting purely on a survival instinct, James clenched his teeth and threw himself toward the other man. He hoped to get his hands on Roth before that gun went off in his face, but wasn't sure if he could do it before Roth had a chance to pull his trigger.

Both men slammed together like two colliding trains. One of them wrapped both arms around the other, even as his lower body exploded in a flood of agony.

James clasped his hands behind Roth's back and started to lift when he felt something smash into him below the belt. There was a second of numbness as the entire world seemed to take a break from spinning.

Then the burning came, followed by a pain so intense that it brought the bile up from his stomach to spill onto the back of his tongue. From there, all James could do was take one step back before dropping down onto the boards and leaning against the nearest wall. Sitting there and looking up at Roth, he could see the other man's knee still raised in the air from where it had pounded into his groin.

"I've had enough of this bullshit," Roth said as he snapped his pistol's hammer back and pointed the barrel at James's face. "Say good night, asshole."

SEVEN

There was one footstep upon the planks of the boardwalk, followed by the low-pitched *whoosh* of something heavy cutting the air. Before anyone could figure out what it was, there was a solid *thump*.

Roth opened his mouth as if to speak, but all that came out was a choking gasp. After that, his eyeballs rolled up into his skull and his entire body teetered to one side. He hung there for a moment, balanced upon the side of one boot, and then toppled over to land in a jumbled heap of sprawling arms and legs.

The surprised look on James's face was identical to the one worn by Frye as both men turned to see exactly what had just happened to bring the confrontation to such a sudden close. They spotted a tall, lean figure with one foot on a step and the other upon the boardwalk itself. In his hand was a smoothly carved piece of wood, which James recognized as one of the axe handles he'd just bought.

Clint swung the axe handle in an easy circle through the air, following the end with his eyes. "There's nothing like a nice piece of hickory," he said.

Once Frye had gotten over the initial shock, he puffed

out his chest and started to reach for one of his guns. "Just who the hell do you think—" But before he could finish, Frye was cut off by the sudden appearance of the tip of the axe handle less than a foot in front of his face.

Holding the blunt club in a steady hand, Clint swung the handle with all of his might, stopping just short of knocking Frye's head into the neighboring county. His steely eyes locked onto Frye and froze the slender man in his tracks.

After a few seconds of tense silence, Frye got up the gumption to speak. "You're making a big mistake, mister."

"Really? Well, shame on me."

"If you know what's good for you, you'd best step aside and tend to your own affairs before you get hurt."

Clint allowed himself a thin smile. "That's a funny thing to hear from a man on the wrong end of this stick."

Frye's eyes showed a fleeting glimpse of fear as he looked to Roth's crumpled body and then back to the axe handle, which remained unmoving directly in front of him. But that fear was short-lived as his own hand tightened around the .38 strapped to his waist.

Twisting his upper body at the waist was all Clint needed to jab the tip of the axe handle against Frye's chin. The knock jarred him, but didn't do any real damage.

"You're not the only one going heeled around here," Clint said in a low, warning voice. "Not anymore."

Reflexively, Frye glanced down to the holster worn by the man directly in front of him. When he heard a groan come from Roth, who was beginning to pull himself to his feet, Frye put his confident smile back in place beneath his finely waxed mustache. "That's right, mister. I'm not the only one with a gun."

Roth was angry enough that he didn't have to hear the order from his boss to jump up and grab hold of the gun that had slipped from his hand. The instant his fingers closed around the pistol's grip, he heard that *whoosh* one more time before Clint's axe handle caught him squarely beneath the chin.

This time, Clint put a little more muscle behind his swing and was already turning back to face Frye as he heard the familiar sound of a body hitting the ground. "He won't be getting up for a while," he said with certainty. "So how about you take what little pride you can salvage and be on your way?"

James didn't know who the man was who'd stepped in on his behalf. All he did know was that, for the first time since this trouble had started, he suddenly found himself on the winning end of a fight. Rather than waste the moment by watching it go by, he snatched the gun from Roth's unconscious hand and brought it up to bear on Frye.

"No need for that," Clint said, recognizing the sound of James snapping back the gun's hammer.

Frye stepped back until he was out of the axe handle's reach. Only then did his smile fully return. It grew even bigger when he heard the door to the neighboring building fly open and another set of boots thumping against the boardwalk.

"I gave you your chance, mister. Just like I gave Jimmy his. Now you're both going to have to pay the price."

Clint spotted a group of men storm out of the building next door, wiping their sleeves across their faces and taking in the scene outside with blatant surprise etched across their features. By the looks of it, they'd been drinking or eating when they heard what was going on and now they were charging to stand at Frye's side.

As soon as he saw that he had plenty of men to back him up, Frye pointed his finger toward Clint and James. "Take them both down," he ordered.

EIGHT

The men emerging from the next storefront over didn't have to hear another word. They were already anxious for action after hearing the sounds of struggle and were even more ready when they came out to see someone threatening the man who paid their salaries.

Clint saw what was coming his way and turned to look at James over his shoulder. "Don't lose your head," he warned. "Follow my lead and don't shoot until we absolutely have to."

"What are you talking about?" James said in an urgent whisper. "They're going to kill us. And who the hell are you, anyway?"

But Clint didn't have enough time to answer James's questions. Instead, he was too busy sprinting toward the oncoming reinforcements before they could get their wits about them enough to be a threat. Clint only needed to take three or four bounding steps before he was close enough to the other men to catch one of them with the axe handle.

Since he didn't know anything more about these men than what Elena had told him, Clint wasn't about to start shooting until he didn't have another choice. Doing so would only turn the whole mess into a bloodbath and turn James Halliwell either into a killer or a corpse.

The first man that Clint could reach was the one who'd been first through the door. Having seen the most of what was going on, that man had already drawn his gun and was about to take a shot when Clint rushed toward him like a rampaging bull.

Using his own momentum, Clint planted one foot and spun his body in a tight circle. When he came around again, he caught sight of the gunman's face a split second before driving the axe handle up against it with a quick, snapping motion.

The impact sounded like a melon had been knocked off a fence post and was enough of a shock to stop the remaining men before they threw themselves toward Clint. By the time the first man had fallen off the boardwalk and landed on the ground below, the rest of Frye's hired hands spread out to try and circle around Clint in an attempt to surround him.

Now that they were all out of the building, Clint could count four of them. Well . . . three, since he doubted the first one would be getting back up anytime soon. The remaining men spread out and watched him with the eyes of experienced fighters. They gauged his movements and didn't try any hasty attacks of their own.

"We can all walk away from this," Clint said. "After all, I've never even seen you boys before in my life."

From what he could see, Clint was every bit the surprise he'd hoped to be. On the way back into town, he realized there might have been the chance that Elena could have talked to someone about her hope to contact him. If that was the case, he thought there might be a chance that whoever was bothering her brother would be ready for someone else to enter the mix. But all of these men seemed surprised enough. James Halliwell, however, seemed more surprised then all of them combined.

"Leave him out of this," James shouted as the other three men began circling Clint. "I don't even know who that man is. Your fight's with me, Frye. Let's keep it that way."

"Oh it's too late for that, Jimmy. Besides, I think I'm going to enjoy this little display very much indeed."

Although Clint admired what James was trying to do, he couldn't allow him to stay where his life was in danger. He hoped that wouldn't be a problem as he said, "Go on and get out of here, James. Your sister's in trouble."

"What?"

"She's waiting by the creek. Go on and make sure Elena's all right. I can handle myself here."

James was visibly torn between two conflicting impulses. On one hand, he didn't want to repay the man who'd saved his life by leaving him on his own. But on the other hand, if his own flesh and blood was in trouble, he'd sworn to protect them no matter what.

"No," James said. He pointed to Frye and added, "if she's in trouble, it's because of that man right there."

Clint had been hoping things wouldn't go this way, but he didn't have much of a choice any more. Especially since one of the hired hands was stepping in to take a swing at him with a knife he'd just pulled from a scabbard at his belt.

Throwing himself back a step, Clint barely managed to avoid getting sliced by the incoming blade. At the same time, he put himself that much closer to the other man who'd moved in behind him. Rather than try to get away from that one as well, Clint tightened his grip on the axe handle and jabbed it straight behind him.

The wider end of the handle buried itself deep into the second man's gut, driving all the air out of him in a noisy rush. Clint followed up by snapping his head back until he felt himself impact against flesh and cartilage.

Staggering backward while clamping his hand to his

nose, the second man groaned in pain as blood poured out from between his fingers. His eyes were wild and unfocused from the pain and he nearly tripped off the edge of the boardwalk to land next to his fallen partner.

Clint looked around at the other two men and saw that the third had stepped back and was drawing his pistol. He'd managed to clear leather just as Clint swung his axe handle in an upward arc, smacking its wooden tip against a pinky finger. The crunch sounded like dry leaves under a boot heel, but there was no mistaking the fact that those dry leaves were in fact small bones.

Even if that man wanted to fire his gun, he would have been unable to do so. In fact, he wasn't even able to keep the pistol from sliding out through his twitching fingers and dropping to the ground at his feet.

That only left one more of Frye's men who was still up and ready to fight. Clint looked at him while swinging the axe handle in a slow circle.

"All right," Clint said. "Now that you have my undivided attention, let's see how well you can do."

The man looked angry enough to charge, but as his eyes flicked down to look at his partners, a bit of hesitancy drifted into him. He started to take a step forward, but stopped. After another half-shuffle, he stopped again to look over toward Frye one last time.

"You want this farmer so bad, then that's fine with me," Frye said. "But believe me, mister, he's more trouble than he's worth."

"Yeah," Clint replied. "I nearly broke this perfectly good piece of lumber."

"That's not the kind of trouble I'm talking about. If you want to see what I mean, you just keep sticking up for Jimmy, here, and you'll have more trouble than you can handle."

Frye locked eyes with Clint for a tense couple of seconds. The well-dressed man gave off a calm presence that was tainted with an undeniable aggression lying just beneath the surface. In those few seconds, Frye sent a definite message that Clint received as clearly as though it had been spoken out loud.

Frye looked toward his only undamaged man and said, "Help those men up, Cobb. We're attracting a crowd."

Sure enough, Clint took a quick look at his surroundings and saw that there were faces peering at the scene from just about every window in sight. Besides that, there were some gathered in small groups along the street, watching intently at what was going on. Clint stepped back and let the men gather themselves up and leave.

Frye didn't even look back as he calmly strolled away.

NINE

James could still feel his heart pounding inside his chest even though Frye and his men seemed to be walking away calmly enough. He held the gun he'd taken in a nervous grip. The longer he held back from pulling the trigger, the more he started to shake in anticipation.

Once the others had gone, Clint rested the axe handle over his shoulder and made his way to James's side. "Put that down before you hurt somebody," he said. When he saw that James was still preparing himself to fire, Clint reached out and gently pushed the other man's hand down until the pistol was pointing toward the ground. "That's better."

Suddenly, James shook his head and blinked his eyes quickly a few times. "Oh my god," he said as though he'd just waken up from a dream. "My sister! You said Evie's in trouble?"

"Relax. I was trying to get you to clear out of here, that's all. Your sister is fine."

James's expression changed again. This time, he fixed Clint with an angry gaze. "You'd best tell me who the hell you are, mister. How do you know my sister?"

Clint was already walking over to the wagon parked in

the street. After tossing the axe handle back to where he'd found it, he started heading for the spot where Eclipse was tied off and waiting for him. "I'll tell you about that over a beer."

Flustered and confused, James ran to his wagon. "But . . . back there. You saved my life."

"Then you're buying." With that, Clint snapped Eclipse's reins and headed for a saloon at the end of the block.

James looked around one more time. He saw Michael Roth being helped to his feet and snarling something under his breath. But since looks alone couldn't do any bodily harm, the gunman wasn't about to start up another fight in the condition he was in. Just to be on the safe side, however, James climbed up onto the wagon and got the horses moving.

He drove straight past the saloon where Clint had gone and took the wagon to a livery. The bulky man working there opened the door for him and helped him down.

"Keep an eye on this for me, will you?" James asked.

The liveryman nodded enthusiastically. "Sure thing, Mister Halliwell. That was a hell of thing that happened just now."

"It sure was," James replied, even though he couldn't quite match the other man's energy.

"Do you know who that man was?" the liveryman asked.

James shook his head. "Nope."

"He sure can fight, though."

"He wants to meet me at Vicker's Saloon. I don't know if I should go or not."

"Why wouldn't you? If it was me, I'd want to shake that man's hand after he damn near took a bullet for me."

"But why would he do such a thing?"

The liveryman shrugged his shoulders and started tending to the horses that had been pulling the wagon. "Who can say? Some folks just want to help. I would've helped you myself, but . . ."

James nodded and pat the other man on the back. He didn't have to hear the rest of what he was going to say to know what words were coming. He would have helped James if he didn't know Frye so well. Most of the people in town had their hearts in the right place, but they didn't want to cross a man like Frye.

"It's all right," James said. Now that his pulse was slowing to a normal pace, his thoughts were coming a whole lot clearer. "I know what you mean. And I think you're right about that stranger. The least I can do to thank him is buy him a drink."

The liveryman smiled. "And when you're done with that, send him my way. I'd pay to see those men get their asses whupped one more time!"

After a few more friendly words, James headed out of the livery and walked toward the nearby saloon. As always, there was the feeling of discomfort in the pit of his stomach whenever he made his way through town. Frye's men were always around, only this time there was something different.

Although James knew he was probably still being watched, he couldn't see any of Frye's thugs glaring at him from a shadow or storefront. For the first time in a while, he didn't hear footsteps trailing him or hear whispered insults hissed at him from the street.

It was like being in the middle of a passing storm. He knew well enough that there was still plenty more rain to come, but it sure felt nice to have some peace and quiet for a spell . . . no matter how short-lived it might be.

TEN

When Clint stepped inside the saloon he'd selected, he had to stop for a moment and stand in the entrance, holding open the loosely hinged door with one hand. The place was about the size of a large house and had plenty of space for people to sit at several small round tables scattered throughout the room. There was even plenty of spots at the twelve-foot-long bar, which was situated along the side of the room.

But Clint still couldn't walk into the place right away because every soul in the saloon had been gathered around the front door and window to get a better view of the street outside. Turning to look over his shoulder, Clint saw that the saloon was in a good position to view the spot where he'd met up with Frye's men minutes ago. In fact, if he squinted, Clint could just make out some of the blood staining the dry ground.

By the time he'd turned back around, most of the locals had cleared a path for him so he could make his way to the bar. There wasn't a raised voice to be heard and every eye within those walls was drilling into the back of Clint's head.

The silence was just starting to get uncomfortable when

Clint set his hands on top of the bar and propped one foot onto the tarnished rail running just above the floor. When he spoke in a quiet voice, the words seemed to echo like thunder.

"Beer, please."

Snapping out of his daze, the chubby barkeep reached for a glass and took it over to the keg that was sitting at the far end of the bar. By the time he'd filled the glass, the rest of the patrons had started talking enough to make the place feel more like a saloon and less like a funeral parlor.

"Sorry about that," the bartender said while setting the beer in front of Clint. "But we couldn't help noticing your little . . . uh . . . scuffle with Mister Frye's boys."

"Thanks for not stepping in or anything," Clint said sarcastically. "Your show might not have lasted so long."

The barkeep stammered for a second or two before deciding to just let that observation pass. "Are you a friend of Mister Halliwell's?"

"I know his sister."

"That would be Evie, I suppose?"

Clint nodded.

Suddenly, the barkeep stopped short and narrowed his eyes. He studied Clint as though he was looking through a magnifying glass and started nodding slowly. "Wait a second . . . I might just remember you."

Clint was only half listening to the bartender since most of his mind was busy wondering what was taking James so long to meet him. In response to what the barkeep was saying, Clint simply nodded and smiled amiably.

"Yeah," the barkeep said while snapping his fingers. "I *do* remember you. Didn't you come through town a year or so back? Kept company with Evie Halliwell."

Since he'd just mentioned Elena's name no more than a minute or so ago, Clint was only partially impressed. "I was here, all right."

The barkeep rubbed his chin and put on a face of exaggerated concentration. "Don't tell me . . . I know I'll remember the name. For some reason, I know I can remember, but . . ." Suddenly, his face lit up. He looked as though he was about to shout something, but then thought better of it and let out a slow breath. "You're Clint Adams."

Clint took a casual look around to see if anyone else had heard that part. He figured that if he was already being studied by the locals here, the mention of his name might cause another surge of whispers. From what he could tell, nobody had heard the barkeep, they didn't recognize his name or they simply weren't impressed.

"That's me, all right," Clint agreed. "You've got a hell of a memory."

"Only for famous men like yerself. It's not every day that a man has the Gunsmith walk into his saloon. I thought the same thing then and I think it now."

By this time, there were definitely a few curious faces turning back in Clint's direction. They might have been reacting to the barkeep's excited tone, but just to be sure, Clint leaned forward and spoke in a casual whisper.

"I think I've had enough attention for one day. Do you think you'd mind just serving my drink and giving me a moment alone?"

The barkeep nodded fervently. "Sure, sure. No problem. I had Bat Masterson in here one time and he kept all to himself at a table in the back, just as quiet as you please. Good thing too, because once folks heard who he was they wouldn't leave him alone with all the questions and staring and—"

"Right. That's the idea," Clint interrupted as he flattened his hand on top of the bar. "I'd really appreciate it." When he lifted his hand up again, he left behind a silver dollar.

Spotting the money and swiping it up with a hand so

fast that it was hardly much more than a greedy blur, the bartender pocketed the coin and winked. "I get ya. My name's Ned. You need anything else, Mister Ad—" Ned stopped himself and lifted a finger to his lips. "Anything else at all . . . you just let me know."

"Will do, Ned. Thanks."

Just then, Clint heard the front door open and close. Turning to look that way, he heard steps heading in his direction. James walked right up to where Clint was standing and took the spot right next to him.

"Hey, Ned. Whatever this man's drinking . . . put it on my tab," James said while hooking his thumb toward Clint. When he noticed what Clint was drinking, he added, "And I'll take one of the same."

The barkeep nodded and filled up another glass.

Neither man said a word until James had his beer and had drained half the glass in one extended gulp. Letting out a breath, James wiped the foam from his upper lip with the back of his sleeve and put the glass back down onto the bar. He wrapped both hands around the glass as though he was afraid it might try to get away from him.

Clint watched all of this carefully. He'd had a few suspicions about the man when he'd first heard about him from Elena. But the more he watched James, the more he became convinced that the other man was pretty much exactly how he appeared.

Noticing that he was once again being studied, James turned toward Clint and asked, "Is something the matter?"

"You look like you could use something a little stronger than beer."

"I could, at that, but I gave up whiskey once I became responsible for my entire family. What about yourself?"

"Beer's fine for me," Clint said. "I guess I just never developed much of a taste for the harder stuff."

James nodded and topped off his beer. After a gesture toward Ned, his glass was refilled and put right back in front of him. "I don't mean to seem ungrateful, but . . . why did you help me back there? And what's it got to do with my sister?"

"Why don't we take a seat over there and talk about it? My feet could use a rest."

James led the way across the saloon and plopped himself down into a chair. Noticing that the other man didn't seem to mind that his back was to the door, Clint sat down with his back to the wall and the door in plain sight. What they said about old habits seemed to have at least some degree of truth.

"All right, James," Clint said, "let's talk. How about you start with why so many hired guns would be after a man like yourself."

ELEVEN

For the most part, the account James told to Clint was pretty much the same as the one he'd heard from Elena. Of course, there were some minor differences, but it wasn't anything that one wouldn't expect from hearing the same story from two different people.

After James was done with his take on things, Clint put both accounts together and came up with a happy medium that was probably the closest thing he could expect to the real thing. James had done his best to make his problems with Frye seem under control, but wasn't doing a good enough job to satisfy his one-man audience.

"I remember Evie talking about you, Mister Adams."

"Call me Clint."

James nodded and took a sip of his beer as though he needed a moment to adjust to the change of names. "She spoke highly of you . . . Clint. I didn't know who you were at first, but she sure did. Tell you the truth, I was kind of relieved that you'd moved on. Nothing personal, but I've heard some things."

"Don't worry about it," Clint said dismissively. "After some of the stories I've heard about myself, I can't say as I'd blame a big brother from being concerned about his little sister being with me."

That, combined with the beer he'd been drinking, put James somewhat at ease. Whatever comfort he took from the quiet moment was quickly gone, however, as his thoughts drifted back to more recent events. "I know how I must look to a man like you, Clint. You must think I'm some kind of coward after seeing me get whipped like a dog in the street."

"You looked like a man who was outnumbered and unwilling to throw himself into a fight with armed men. That doesn't make you cowardly in anyone's book." After taking a sip of his own beer, Clint added, "A little unlucky, perhaps, but not a coward."

This time, James's smile lasted more than just a few seconds. He shook his head and leaned back in his chair, looking more relaxed than he had the entire time they'd been in the saloon. "As much as I'd like to argue about that, I couldn't do it in good conscience. My luck's been lower than a snake's belly for a while now."

"And that all started when Frye took an interest in that ranch of your father's?"

"Pretty much. Once he got it in his head that he wanted that property, there wasn't a damn thing anyone could say to change his mind."

"What about the money he's offering?"

"It's got to be less than a third of what it's worth," James answered in a voice that was just barely above a whisper. "Mister Frye don't even know the meaning of a square deal. I never told Evie this, but that land's even more valuable than the stock that grazes on it. A hell of a lot more."

"Why? Did the railroad make an offer to build through there?"

James shook his head. "Nothing like that."

"Then what? I didn't think Nebraska was known too much for gold or mining."

"Not particularly. It's mostly farms and prairie out that way."

Leaning back and holding his beer, Clint thought for a moment. His curiosity had genuinely been peaked. "I give up, then. Why's that land so valuable?"

Propping both elbows upon the table, James looked across at Clint with a glint in his eye. "The man who left that ranch to our family used to live down in Texas."

"Kyle Bagley, I know," Clint interrupted. "Elena told me about that part."

"Well, she probably didn't tell you that Bagley was partners with another man down there by the name of Peyton Lowry. Mister Lowry had visited the ranch a few times and admired the spread. Even offered to buy it outright, but he could never get Bagley to sell."

Even though James was looking at him as though he'd just let some big secret spill out, Clint had no idea what that secret was. He waited for James to go on, but only got expectant silence in return.

"Don't tell me you're finished," Clint said. "Because I'm still not following where you're going with this."

"Have you ever known any rich men, Clint?"

"A few."

"What about rich men from Texas?"

Suddenly, a dim light started to appear in the darkness. "I spend a lot of time in Texas, sure."

"Then maybe you know how those men got rich. Once they set their sights on something, they never forget about it until they've got it or they decide they don't want it anymore. And if they hear they *can't* have something . . . they act like a dog holding onto a bone being pulled from its mouth."

Clint nodded slowly. "*Now* I'm starting to see where this is headed."

"Well, every time Peyton Lowry heard the word *no* from Bagley, he wanted that spread for himself more and more. Who the hell knows why he wants it so bad," James said. "It could be for the view or the stock it puts out. It could just be a feather in his cap, but whatever the reason is, he's brought the price up to forty thousand."

"I've heard of Peyton Lowry," Clint said. "Some say he makes Bagley look like a homesteader. He could afford that much for a whim. And you're right about those cattle barons. They'll go further to prove a point than most men would go to save their lives. How did you find out so much about all of this? If Bagley was so dead-set against selling, I wouldn't think he'd want all of this to get out."

"You've got that right. But once Bagley died, Lowry was spouting off to anyone he could find about wanting to buy that property."

"Especially once he realized that it wasn't left to him, I'll bet."

James nodded and grinned. "He was plenty worked up that he didn't get his hands on that deed. Lowery made his offer to anyone and everyone who might know who did get the legal rights to the place."

"Why wasn't it ever sold?"

"You got me. I never even knew my father had the deed until he was on his deathbed. He said he kept it to make sure we would all be taken care of after he was gone. All Frye wants to do is sell it outright."

"And what about you?"

Leaning back, James looked up toward the ceiling as though he saw his entire future drawn across the dusty beams. "I plan on running the place myself. Once I get out there, I can see for myself what makes that spread so valuable. After that, I can either work it up or sell it back to Mister Lowry for what it's really worth. Either way, I'll come out a whole lot better than if I take whatever Frye's offering. Hell, Frye would just as soon kill me as soon as he got the deed rather than pay. At least Mister Lowry is a legitimate businessman."

"I've got some bad news for you, James. Most men as rich as Lowry don't get that way by being completely legitimate."

"Hell, I know that. But my father always told me that a man's a whole lot more secure in his life if he handles things his own way. However things turn out, at least he can live with himself."

"Your father sounds like a smart man," Clint said.

James looked down into his glass while swirling its contents around. His eyes took on a faraway quality as he slowly started to nod. "He sure was."

TWELVE

"That boy's father was a goddamn fool!"

The moment Zeke Frye got into the back room he used for an office, his polished exterior came tumbling down to reveal the seething rage that had been lying in wait just beneath the surface. After he spouted out that last statement, he punctuated it by slamming his hand flat against the top of his desk.

"If old man Halliwell had had one ounce of brains in his head, he might have been dangerous. When he was alive, he wasn't good at anything but getting underfoot. He's dead now and he's still managing to jam up the works."

The only other man in the room sat halfway slumped in an old couch, which reeked of mothballs and cigarette smoke. He held a wet cloth to his jaw and cringed at the pain that just putting it there sent through his face. Sucking in a deep breath, Roth held it for a second or two and then let it out through tightly clenched teeth.

"Then why keep pussyfooting around with the fool's son?" Roth asked. "Give me the word and I'll make it so that not even James's family will be able to recognize him."

"That won't fix the big picture, though. If we kill him outright, the deed to that ranch will probably just go to his mother or sister."

Roth spat out a wad of blood and rubbed a sore spot on his jaw. "I can solve that problem, too."

Frye had been pacing back and forth across the room's biggest window. His hands were clasped behind his back and his feet hit the floor as though he had a personal grudge against every board. "Killing every last one of those bastard Halliwells might make us all feel better, but they might burn the deed before it's all said and done.

"Breaking Halliwell is the simplest way to get what I want. He was close to giving in. I could feel it. We were that close," Frye said while holding his thumb and fore-finger a quarter of an inch apart. "And then . . ."

Too angry to finish the sentence, Frye clenched every finger on that hand into a fist and slammed it through the wall beside the window. His knuckles broke a large hole into the wall. Chunks of broken, bloody wood dropped to the floor and stuck to the tattered, shredded skin of Frye's hand.

Roth was unimpressed by his boss's angry display. When Frye's fist made a hole in one of the walls, the gunman didn't even flinch. He seemed more affected by the noise of the crash, which echoed painfully inside his throbbing skull.

"Do you know who that fella was who stepped in for Jim?" Roth asked.

Frye glared up from his bloody hand and fixed his eyes upon the other man. "Funny . . . I was just about to ask you the same thing."

Roth shrugged. "I had a talk with Ned over at Vicker's Saloon. He said it was Clint Adams, himself. Do you think Jim might've hired him?"

Pausing to think about that for a moment, Frye walked across his office and picked up a towel from a tray of drinks that had been sitting there since his morning coffee. Dabbing the towel against his knuckles, he said, "Could be. Who gives a shit? I don't care if it was the Gunsmith or Jesus Christ, he don't get away with working over my men with an axe handle."

Roth got to his feet and rolled his head in a slow circular motion. Along with all the pops and cracks, he could feel his blood coursing through his veins. The pain was still there, but it wasn't anything that he couldn't handle.

"You all right?" Frye asked.

"Yeah."

"Good. Because if I ever see anyone get the drop on you so easily again, I'll have to think real hard about why I keep you around."

Roth's eyes flared and his words came out in a fierce snarl. "That son of a bitch snuck up on us. He got lucky. That's all."

"You can say whatever you want about the how's, but that don't change the what's."

As much as he hated to admit it, Roth couldn't argue with his employer's point. That fact hurt much more than any of the bumps or bruises he sported. Fortunately, a man's pride was relatively easy to fix so long as he was willing to go to any lengths.

"When I kill Adams," Roth said, "I'll make it real messy. That'll keep anyone else from getting any smart ideas. I still say I should take them Halliwells out while I'm at it."

With the blood soaking into the towel and turning the white cotton a dark crimson, Frye's temper seemed to be easing off. His breaths were more controlled and his voice had lost its unsteady waver. "The more I think about it, the more I think you just may have a point there."

"You're taking an awful big risk by letting that farmer live."

"Taking risks is why I get the biggest share of the profits."

Knowing he wasn't about to get any further with the man, Roth shook his head again and walked out the door.

THIRTEEN

Although he was offered another round of complimentary beer, Clint decided to hold off on accepting James's hospitality in favor for a cup of cold water. He was far from drunk, but in light of his current situation, Clint figured it was best all around if he kept his senses as sharp as possible.

James Halliwell seemed to be thinking along those similar lines. "I appreciate what you did for me, Clint. But I don't think it's over between me and Mister Frye."

"I just got into town and I can tell you for a fact that it's not over."

Sighing heavily, James nodded slowly. The weight that had been lifted temporarily from his shoulders was suddenly back. "Yeah. I figured as much."

"Did your father put something in your head to get you so set in your ways, James?"

"Set in my ways? Frye is threatening me, my family and our well-being. I don't have any choice but to defend myself. And them. I thought you understood that."

Clint leaned forward just enough so that he didn't have to raise his voice loud enough to be heard by anyone else. Even though the rest of the saloon seemed to be content with leaving them alone for the moment, Clint still caught some of the other patrons trying to catch a word or two to fuel their own rumor-laden conversations.

"I understand well enough, James. It sounds like your father was trying to play things right by keeping this place under his hat. There might be more to that place than you know."

James nodded. "Maybe, but my mother's been after me to put that deed away and forget about it. She acts like it's cursed or something."

'Hiding the deed was a smart thing to do, since your father probably figured that there would always be someone out to cash in for themselves.

"If it wasn't Frye, it would have been someone else looking to get rich quick. The point I'm trying to make is that . . ." Clint paused for a second to think about what he wanted to say before he said it. Unable to come up with a delicate way to phrase his words, he just spit them out the best he could. "The point is that you're going about this the wrong way."

"What do you mean?"

"Well, you're trying to do the right thing, but if you keep on the way you're going, the only thing you're going to get out of it is a spot in the ground. You're not much of a fighting man."

James clenched his fists, but kept himself from pounding them upon the table. A curse formed on the tip of his tongue, but he also kept himself from spitting it at Clint. Instead of any of these things, he said, "I'm doing the best that I know, Mister Adams."

"I know, but I can tell you right now that Frye's been playing easy with you."

"Easy?" James said while pointing up to the bruises on his face. "You call this easy?"

"Yes. I do. Those bruises could be bullet holes. You've got eyes, so that also means that you probably saw those guns hanging from those belts they were wearing."

"And I also saw the gun being pointed in my face before you came along."

"Which brings me back to what I was saying before. You got lucky. As far as me coming along when I did, you can thank your sister for that."

The anger James felt was plain enough to see in his eyes. It faded, however, the more he thought about what Clint was saying. Somewhere inside, he must have decided that Clint was telling the truth. That didn't help his bruised and battered pride, however.

"If Frye wanted you dead, he could have done it several times over by now. I don't have to see more than what I saw to tell you that much. What about the law here? Did you ever go to them?"

"Yeah," James replied. "But this is a small town. Sheriff Williams does the best job he can do, but if any of Frye's men wind up in a cell, they're out before the day's up. Frye just owns too much of Barryville to be concerned with the law."

Clint nodded. He'd expected to hear something along those lines even before he'd finished his question. Small towns were a lot like a tract of wild land. All a man had to do was take a look at which dog strutted the most to tell who was in charge. Also, the fact that the entire fight Clint had been in had gone on without a single badge making their presence known.

"I don't mean to talk down to you," Clint said. "But when I first saw what was happening to you, my guts told me that you were in this over your head."

"Much as I hate to admit it . . . I'd say your guts were right this time."

"Then if we're going to change the way this plays out, you're going to have to change the way you operate. Frye and his men get their edge because a normal man doesn't think like a wild animal, which is all those killers are.

That's all Frye is and knowing that is the first step to beating them."

James stared intently at Clint, soaking up every word that he said.

"The first thing you've got to do is watch yourself." Clint pointed over James's shoulder toward the front door. "Frye or any of those others could have walked in here any time. And if they did, the first thing they'd see is your back. You don't put your back to a killer with a gun, James. Not if you want to stay alive."

Nodding, James glanced toward the door and changed his position at the table so he could get a better look at the saloon's door.

Clint watched him and noticed that James already seemed to have a more watchful air about him. Besides that, there was also a little more fear showing through in his eyes. "That's good. Now, all I'm asking is that you keep your wits about you. I'm not about to be your body-guard, but we can get these men if we're both on the lookout. Don't make it easy for them. That should hold them off long enough for us to take care of this business of yours."

"Long enough for *us*?" James asked hopefully.

Nodding, Clint said, "That's right. I'm in this now, too. That is, if you don't mind the intrusion."

James's beaming smile was all the answer Clint needed.

FOURTEEN

Clint talked to James for another half hour or so. Mostly, he was just trying to make sure that the eldest male Halliwell didn't go off and try to do something foolish in a desperate attempt to protect his family. Although he couldn't fault the man for his reasons, Clint knew that Frye might very well be ready to do some desperate actions of his own since James might just have become more trouble than he was worth.

Of course, Clint also knew that that was due mainly to the fact that he'd stepped in on James's behalf.

Sometimes, Clint had to wonder if he wasn't the cause of all these problems he constantly encountered. It wasn't a notion that he seriously considered, but it was always in the back of his mind whenever he came across yet another person in dire straights.

It had been happening for years. The closest Clint could ever come to an explanation was that he was just one of the few men out there who had his eyes open and could do something to right the wrongs he saw. He didn't fancy himself any kind of hero. Especially since his original intentions had been anything but noble when he'd made his way toward Barryville. That is, unless spending another hot night or two with James's sister was considered noble these days.

Rather than bother himself with such technicalities, Clint did his best to put James on the right track so that Frye didn't get the opportunity to end their feud with a single shot in the dark.

"All of this may sound like a lot to bear," Clint said once they'd started to wrap things up. "But all you have to do is stay out of trouble until this blows over."

"And when is that going to happen?"

"As soon as dealing with you becomes more trouble than it's worth to Frye or you unload that ranch. Either way, I'll do what I can to find out which trail is the one we should take and do my best to see you get to the end of it in one piece."

That made James feel even better. He laughed a bit to himself and nodded in approval. "Sounds great, Clint. In fact, we might not even have to worry about Frye no more."

"Excuse me?"

"I mean . . . you're on my side now and you're . . . well . . . Clint Adams."

"I'm trying to do this in a way that will keep too many shots from getting fired. Believe me, being who I am won't scare Frye off. If anything, it might even cause some of his men to come after you even harder. You need numbers on your side to scare off a pack of wild dogs like Frye's bunch. If the shooting starts early, it'll just put too many innocent people in the crossfire."

"You're right." James sighed. "I guess I was just hoping to get this over with a little quicker."

"Tell you what," Clint said while checking his pocket watch. "It's getting late." Taking a second look at the timepiece, he added, "Actually, it's not all that late, but I feel like we've been talking about this all day long. Why don't you go home and get some rest."

"But I've still got chores to do and supplies to get."

"Then finish up and head home."

James bristled slightly like a dog with its hackles up. "You think there'll be any more trouble?"

"Could be, but I doubt it. Frye's probably thinking about what he means to do next and his men are licking their wounds. Just let me worry about them."

"But I want to help. After all they've done, I can't just—"

"You can just do what I say and stay alive," Clint interrupted in a steely, straight-edged tone. "Right now, those gunmen can smell how much you want to take them on. They've probably been able to smell it since the first time they started stirring all of this shit up. But if you play their game, the only thing you'll do is die on their terms."

"And what if I don't get much of a choice?"

"If that's the case, then you do what you need to survive. I'm not saying that you don't use that gun you took, but just don't put yourself in a bad situation." Pausing for a moment, Clint took some of the intensity from his voice. "Just don't do anything stupid, James. That's all I'm asking."

"I might not have done things the best way I could," James said. "But it was the only way I could think of. I've been listening to what you said and I'll do my best to see it through."

"That's all I can ask. I just hope I'm pointing you in the right direction."

"You mentioned going with your gut feeling. Well, my gut tells me that you know what you're talking about." James reached out to shake Clint's hand. "I'll try to watch where I'm going for a bit, but I can't guarantee that I'll back down if any of those bastards come at me again."

Since that was the best that Clint expected to get out of James for the time being, he shook the other man's hand and said, "That sounds fair enough. And don't worry about the rest of your family. I know where to find your sister and I'll make sure she's all right. After that, I'll check in on the rest of them."

"I wish I knew how to thank you, Clint. I honestly do."

In response to that, Clint simply nodded. He watched as James headed out of the saloon and noticed that the other man did seem to be watching his step a bit more than before. He was literally glancing from side to side and studying his surroundings before taking his next step.

Although Clint hadn't meant for his directions to be taken so much to heart, he figured it was better all around for James to be more cautious if that meant keeping him safe. When James was gone, Clint got up and took a look around for himself. While none of the locals were blatantly staring at him, it was obvious that they were all watching him from the corners of their eyes.

Good, Clint thought.

Part of the reason he'd taken so long to speak with James was to beat into his head how dangerous his situation had become. But more than that, Clint figured that he would be sending a message at the same time.

There had to be at least one or two folks inside the saloon who would report back to Frye. And when they did, they would have surely gotten wind of who Clint was as well as what he was doing. Such a spy was the perfect messenger for Clint's purposes.

The message they were delivering was simple.

Frye was no longer pushing around a well-meaning working man. He had to contend with someone else now, and the Gunsmith was known for pushing back.

FIFTEEN

When she'd first watched Clint ride off into town, Elena had planned on staying put and waiting for him to return, just as she'd been instructed. It was only natural enough, she figured, that she wanted to follow after him a little ways just so she could see what he was doing. After all, it was her brother in danger.

Once she found herself far enough away from where she was supposed to wait, she then figured it couldn't do any more harm to go the rest of the way. She'd been just in time to see Frye and his men storming away from her family's wagon. By the looks of things, the gunmen had taken a solid beating.

She suddenly felt her concern for James rising to feverish heights as she began to wonder just how bad the fight had left him. After everything that had happened, she knew better than to even hope that the fight they'd been in hadn't involved James.

As luck would have it, she was just crossing the street when she caught sight of Clint riding up to Vicker's Saloon. Not too long after that, James followed. Since both of the men seemed to be looking for someone other than herself, Elena managed to keep herself out of sight until they'd entered the saloon.

Relieved, she waited outside the place until they came out. She was anxious to hear what happened, but when they didn't emerge right away, she peeked in through a window to find Clint and James engaged in some kind of heated conversation. Whatever they were saying, Elena was just glad that Clint was still there. And rather than wait for them any longer, she headed back toward the edge of town so she could be there once Clint was finally ready to seek her out.

It was right about then that she started to get the feeling that she wasn't alone on the lonely street, which stretched beyond the Barryville limits to become a wandering dirt path. Having lived there most of her life, her ears had become accustomed to every last noise, no matter how subtle, that filled the familiar air.

She knew the sound of the insects chirping in summer as well as the wind blowing in the fall. And she most definitely knew the sound of footsteps trailing not too far behind her. The only thing she didn't know was what she was going to do about them.

Taking in a deep breath, Elena gathered her strength and spun around on the balls of her feet. A vicious threat was prepared and waiting at the back of her throat. She came to a stop and was ready to launch her verbal attack when she saw a face that made the words catch before they saw the other side of her teeth.

"By the look on your face, I can't tell if you were about to scream or take a swing at me," Clint said as he raised his arms as if to block an incoming blow.

Elena felt her heart racing within her chest and the adrenaline coursing through her veins. Her fists were balled up and she had to give Clint at least one halfhearted smack to alleviate the tension. "It was almost both," she scolded. "Dammit, Clint you scared the life out of me!"

"I thought I told you to stay put and I'd come back for you."

"I know but . . ." Stopping herself in mid-explanation, she narrowed her eyes and smacked Clint lightly once again. "Don't change the subject like that. I swear you've given me a few gray hairs just now."

Clint reached out and ran his fingers gently through the dark brown hair that framed her face. The strands felt smooth and silky against his skin and nearly all the anger in her face was gone by the time he pulled his arm back again.

"I don't see any gray," he said. "At least, not right there."

Stepping in closer, Elena whispered, "Then perhaps you should keep looking."

That was all Clint needed to hear before he leaned down so that his lips were almost brushing against her temple. Using both hands, he combed his fingers through her hair until he was able to lightly massage the back of her head.

"Mmm," she purred. "That's nice."

When Clint spoke, his lips barely grazed Elena's skin. His breath sent warm tremors just beneath her flesh. "It sure is. Just like I remember."

He took the next few moments to continue moving his hands through her hair. Although it was a simple thing, Clint couldn't seem to get enough of the perfect softness that flowed through his fingers. He also savored the little contented noises she would make in response to his touch, as well as the way she slowly moved her body against him.

It wasn't easy, but Elena somehow got herself to think about something else besides the feel of Clint touching her. "What—what happened in town?" she asked. "I thought there was a fight."

"There was," Clint said. "But it's over now."

Normally, that would have upset Elena to hear such a thing. But coming from Clint, it didn't seem so bad. "Is James all right?"

"Yes."

His fingers brushed along the back of her neck, sending chills all the way down her spine.

"What happens now?"

Clint stepped around so that he was once again behind her. His hands moved so that they were caressing the front of her neck, brushing slowly over the upper curve of her breasts. "Now, we sit tight and go about our business. Frye's got enough to think about for a while. He won't be back until he's digested it."

"Are you sure about that?"

Clint nodded. "As sure as I can be. Frye will be back, but not right away. Besides . . . right now, I'm the one he wants."

Reaching up to place her hands on top of Clint's, Elena moved his hands lower until she could feel his palms brushing her nipples through the material of her dress. Pressing herself back against him, she could also feel his erection pressing against her buttocks.

"Then it looks like me and Frye have something in common," she said softly.

SIXTEEN

Peeling herself away from Clint's body almost pained Elena to do so, but it was an exciting, tingling sort of sensation that felt like a fire burning deeply within her. She took Clint's hands inside her own and started pulling him farther down the path.

"What are you doing?" Clint asked.

"You'll see. Just follow me."

The smell of Elena's skin was still flowing through Clint's nostrils. All he could think about was the feel of her body and the touch of her hair. At the moment, he didn't care if there was an army of killers nearby waiting to gun him down. In fact, the thought of that danger only made his body ache more for her and it was all he could do to keep himself from tearing her clothes off and throwing her down right then and there.

It made Clint's discomfort worse when he realized that Elena probably would have let him do exactly that with a seductive smile on her face.

Elena knew exactly what she was doing to him. In fact, she savored every bit of the energy that flowed between them as she pulled Clint away from the trail and dodged his repeated attempts to get a better hold on her. Leading him through a stand of bushes and between a couple tall trees, she finally stopped and turned around to face him.

"Do you think any of Frye's men are after us?" she asked.

While Clint was still feeling the intense desire for Elena, he was getting more uneasy with that very question. "There could be."

"Then why don't you make sure? I'll be waiting for you right here when you're done."

The part of Clint's brain that was practical thought that was a very good idea. But the rest of him, along with all of his body, didn't want to let her out of his sight for a moment. Fortunately, the part with the common sense won out and Clint managed to work his way back around to the trail so that he could spot anyone who had been moving in behind them.

As far as he could tell, there was nobody on the trail either ahead or behind their last position. Keeping as much to the shadows as he could, Clint headed toward town while scanning everything around him from the rooftops to the alleyways.

He didn't bother scouting too far into town, otherwise he knew there was a chance he might pick up a follower along the way. Turning around and retracing his steps, Clint satisfied himself that his initial notion had been correct and Frye wasn't about to send in his men after freshly getting themselves beaten down the last time.

In the time it took for him to get to the spot where he'd left Elena waiting, Clint was staring to think that he should just take her home and make sure she was out of any possible danger. After all, that was what he'd drilled into James's head less than half an hour ago. Just because there weren't any gunmen after them right this instant, didn't mean that they weren't on their way.

Clint thought about all of this as he stepped through the bushes and between the trees. Just before stepping into the small clearing that Elena had shown him, he'd even managed to convince himself that taking her home was exactly the right thing to do.

Then . . . he stepped through the leafy cover and saw what was waiting for him.

Elena was leaning against the thick trunk of a tree with one leg propped up on the bark. The only thing she wore was her long, dark red coat, which was made of a material that was slightly thinner than her dress. That dress was draped on a bush after being thrown there in a rush. Her boots were laying on the ground below.

When she saw him coming, Elena smiled warmly and slipped her hands down along her hips, pushing open the coat to reveal the smooth, voluptuous contours of her naked body. Her breasts were firm and round, capped with small, dark nipples that became harder as Clint got closer. Her stomach heaved as her breaths quickened. Diverting her hands inward, she traced an inviting line around the dark patch of hair between her legs.

"I've been waiting for you," she whispered.

Clint moved up until he was close enough to reach out and place a hand on either of her hips. "And without any bells on, I see."

Elena smiled and arched her back. Leaning her head so that it rested against the tree as well, she squirmed slowly as Clint's hands moved up and down along her sides. Her nipples were erect little nubs by now and she let out a deep breath as soon as Clint's fingers brushed against them.

"There's nobody coming," Clint said.

Without opening her eyes, Elena slid one hand between Clint's legs and said, "We'll just see about that."

SEVENTEEN

Clint shed his jacket and shirt while Elena stroked him through his jeans. All the while, he let his eyes wander over her smooth, naked skin. There was just enough of a chill in the air to bring out a light dusting of goose bumps on her flesh, but she still seemed warm enough when he got his hands back on her hips.

"This reminds me of old times," she said.

"I have a feeling we won't be thinking about the past for much longer." Sliding one hand around to cup her buttocks, Clint placed the other hand between Elena's legs and began stroking the lips of her vagina in a slow, gentle rhythm.

Her eyes closed and she arched her back even more, pressing her hands against the tree behind her as Clint's fingers slipped into her warm folds. Ripples of pleasure coursed throughout her entire body, bringing her almost instantly to the climax that had been building ever since she'd first gotten him alone.

Her body was still shuddering when Clint took his hand away from her and stepped back. The moment she opened her eyes, Elena looked at Clint hungrily. She grabbed hold

of him and nearly tore the jeans off his body in her haste
to get him undressed before her.

Once she'd managed to slide his pants down, she knelt
in front of Clint and flicked her tongue out against his
thigh. She made sure that her hair brushed against his skin
while her lips traced a warm path up to his erect penis.

Clint reached down and once again let his fingers wander through Elena's hair. All he had to do was gently
guide her toward him and she was wrapping her lips
around the tip of his cock, her tongue swirling around the
sensitive skin.

She teased him for no longer than a second or two
before taking him all the way into her mouth. Reaching
around to pull Clint even closer, she sucked on him vig-
orously and then pulled her head back almost far enough
for him to slip out. Before that could happen, she swallowed him again. This time, however, she bobbed her
head back and forth while caressing him with her tongue.

Keeping his hands on the back of her head, Clint let
out a soft moan as Elena slid him in and out of her mouth.
When he was able to get his wits about him again, he
pulled back and helped her to her feet.

Looking up at him while breathing heavily, Elena
wrapped one hand around his cock and started stroking
him. She felt his hands wrap around her body and with a
little hop, she was off the ground and in his arms. Her
legs wrapped tightly around his waist and she locked her
fingers behind Clint's neck.

With the blood pumping so quickly through his body,
it took hardly any effort at all for Clint to lift Elena up
and walk with her to the edge of the small clearing. He
had his eye on the same tree that she'd been leaning on
before and when he was there, Clint put Elena's back
against the sturdy bark and supported her with one hand,
cupping her small, plump buttocks.

Elena's eyes widened with excitement and she adjusted

herself so that her body was comfortably pressed against his. Keeping her feet wrapped tightly around him, she spread her legs just a little wider until she felt Clint's rigid shaft grinding against the wet lips of her vagina.

Feeling himself rub against the smooth skin between Elena's legs was pleasurable enough. But when Clint slid inside of her and thrust his hips forward, he felt as though the entire clearing was spinning around him.

Once he'd buried himself in as far as he could go, he stayed put for a moment and let the sensations wash over him. He could feel Elena's heart beating against his bare chest and her nails digging into his shoulders. She moaned softly in his ear as he started moving in and out of her. Those moans became louder and more insistent when he began pumping forcefully between her thighs.

Elena started to cry out louder, but kept the words from slipping out since she knew they would probably be heard by some of the people on the outer edge of town. Rather than indulge herself fully, she bit down on her lower lip and pushed the screams back down into her chest. The effort made every one of Clint's thrusts more intense.

Driving all the way inside of her one last time, Clint stepped back and took a breath.

"What's the matter?" Elena asked breathlessly. "Why did you stop?"

"My legs . . . they're getting weak," Clint said as he set her down onto her own two feet.

Elena smiled broadly and lowered herself back down to her knees. Pulling him down by the hands, she said, "Then get down here."

Clint did just that and sat on the soft ground.

Straddling his waist, she said, ". . . lay back . . ." Elena pressed her palms onto Clint's chest and pushed him back. ". . . and let me do all the work."

Already, Clint felt as though he could pick her back up and take her back to his own hotel room, but her plan sounded better and better with each passing moment. So he stretched out on the ground and let Elena climb on top of him.

She straddled his waist and took him in one hand. Guiding his cock between her legs, she fit it into her pussy and lowered herself the rest of the way down. From there, she rode him while straightening her back and running her hands down along her hips. As her rhythm became more intense, she seemed to lose herself in the moment, allowing her head to lean back even further in a way that pressed her full breasts out in an erotic display.

Clint felt his own climax quickly approaching and grabbed Elena by the waist to guide her motions in just the right way. She took the directions naturally, allowing Clint to get her rocking back and forth as well as up and down.

Neither of their systems could take much more and finally, both of them were swept away in a surge of pure sensation. Clint's grip on Elena's waist tightened and he thrust upward one final time before exploding inside of her.

She, too, was on the cusp of another orgasm and all it took to push her over the edge was the feel of Clint's shaft rubbing perfectly against her sensitive skin. At the last moment, she reached down to slide her fingers between her legs, feeling where his body entered her own. Before her fingers could move away, she was trembling and moaning in the back of her throat.

Then, both of them felt all their strength drain from their muscles.

For the next couple of moments, Clint and Elena lay on the ground beneath the stars, their naked bodies still entwined and joined at the hip. Neither one could speak. In fact, neither one wanted to speak.

They simply laid in each other's arms, gazing up at the sky. For the time being, Clint forgot about everything that had happened since he'd arrived. None of that seemed to matter. At least . . . not right then, anyway. The only thing that mattered was that he could still feel Elena's naked body against his own.

After a few minutes, he started to stir.

"We'd best get going," Clint said.

Elena sat up but didn't make the first move toward her clothes. "Well if any of Frye's boys were watching us, at least we gave them a hell of a show."

Clint couldn't help but laugh as he stepped into his jeans.

EIGHTEEN

Michael Roth didn't feel the slightest bit hurried by the insistent tone of his employer's voice. He left Frye's office when he was good and ready, not giving a damn how much Frye wanted to get cracking on the task of breaking the Halliwells down. As far as that went, Roth had plenty of his own plans for accomplishing that particular goal.

Even beyond what Frye had in mind, Roth was working on his own plans that concerned him far more than anything else. The longer he worked with Frye, the more Roth thought the other man was nothing but a skinny pimp in a dandy's clothes. Frye's brain seemed to be wrapped around manipulating people and making himself look big.

In Roth's mind, that was a pimp's job.

A real man didn't have to make himself look big. All he had to do was whatever came naturally and a man's true nature would show. Roth never believed that more than after he'd started working for Frye. Once he'd stood back and watched that one's nature shine through, Roth was convinced he needed to make his own plans if he was going to be something outside of this two-bit town.

In order to do that, Roth needed to do whatever came

naturally. And for a real man, that was taking the world by the throat and squeezing until it dropped whatever it was you were after.

To that end, Roth strutted out of Frye's office like a man on a mission. He left the small building and crossed the street, filling every one of his steps with fire and purpose. When he passed a group of pasty-faced locals, they all cleared a path for him. If he looked in their direction, they quickly looked away.

They knew he wasn't just another one of Frye's lapdogs. They knew he wasn't just some small-town pimp, either. Every damn person in that town knew that Michael Roth was a force to be reckoned with.

Keeping that in mind, Roth made a line straight across town for the Hilltop Lodge. The men he wanted to see had been staying there for a few weeks now and they could afford to rent out the best suite in the place. Roth ignored the man behind the front desk and stormed up the stairs to the third floor.

There was only two rooms up there, but each one of them was bigger than the home where Roth and his four siblings had grown up. A narrow hallway lined with fine red carpeting went down the entire length of the building. There was a window at each end and one door on either side. His feet thumping heavily against the floorboards, Roth passed the first door and stopped at the second.

He lifted a fist to the smoothly sanded door and was about to pound upon it with enough force to rattle it upon its hinges. But Roth took a moment to pull back.

These men weren't the kinds that Frye was used to. They didn't hide in shadows or respond well to strong-arm tactics. They needed to be finessed, which was something that a pimp simply wasn't capable of doing.

Rather than rap upon the door, Roth knocked his knuckles against the wood. After all, he figured, there was no need to bother ruffling their feathers just yet. He'd deal with them like a man . . . right up until it was time to show them who the real boss was.

Just when Roth was about to knock again, he saw the circular brass plate set into the upper section of the door move aside. Peering out from behind the polished metal ring was a large, unblinking eye.

"Yeah?" a muffled voice grunted from the other side of the door.

Roth glared right back at that eye until he saw it blink. Only then did he answer. "I'm here to see Evans."

"Who are you?"

"Just tell him Michael Roth wants to see him. And be quick about it."

Satisfied that he'd put just the right amount of force in his voice, Roth held the eye's gaze until the brass plate slid back into place. He could hear more muffled voices and a few footsteps. Feeling a bitter taste well up in the back of his throat after too much time had passed, Roth started reaching for the door's handle when it turned on its own and swung inward.

Standing just inside the suite was a man who almost filled out the entire space of the frame. Even though the spy hole had been slightly higher than Roth's eye level, the man who'd opened the door had obviously had to bend down to look through it. Dressed in a pressed white shirt and plain black pants, the seven-foot brute gave Roth a stare of his own and held out one pawlike hand.

"Your gun," the giant said. "Hand it over."

Despite the fact that Roth had never personally seen a man as large as this one, he didn't let his eyes waver in the slightest. Holding his ground, he placed his hand upon the handle of his .45 and kept it there. "I'll hand your own ass to you before I hand over this gun," he snarled.

Grinning slightly, the giant looked over his shoulder and waited.

"It's all right, Bullock," came another voice from deep within the suite. "Let him in here."

When the big man moved, he did so with slow precision. It was plain to see by the way his clothes strained over his bulk that he was made up mostly of muscle. Not one part of him looked anything but rock-solid as he stepped aside. His lungs huffed like the deep breaths of a bison.

By the way he walked past the bigger man, Roth acted as if he'd been the one to back the giant down. He did an admirable job of maintaining his intense stare as he walked through the doorway and into the plush hotel suite.

The inside of the room was as different from the rest of the entire town as summer was different from winter. Judging by the full, rich carpeting and exquisite paintings adorning every wall, the suite might very well have been plucked from downtown San Francisco and dropped onto the top of the lodge.

Nowhere else in Barryville were there so many smooth corners and finely crafted works. The mirrors were edged in crystal and every frame was streaked with gold. Even the glasses next to the whiskey tumbler by the door were impressive.

And sitting in the middle of it all, reclining on a comfortable chair as though it was his throne, sat a man in his late forties wearing an expertly tailored suit. What little hair that was still on his head formed a dark ring around the edge of his scalp and was greased against the surface of his skull.

He smiled as if to display his perfectly aligned teeth and waved for Roth to step forward. "Come on in," he said with a sharp Texas twang. "Don't let Bullock scare you. He don't break anyone unless I give him the word."

From most people, Roth would take that as bluster. But after seeing the size of Bullock and the wealth displayed within this room, Roth had no trouble believing that the big man would rip a preacher in two if his master snapped his fingers the right way.

The well-dressed man got up from his throne and took a sip from the glass in his hand. "And don't get yourself too worked up, Bull," he said to the giant. "I'm sure our guest here can see it would be in his best interest to mind his manners."

Hearing that, Roth looked around and saw no fewer than half a dozen men sitting or standing at various spots around the suite. Every one of them wore pistols in plain view strapped to their sides. They moved like predatory cats, every step taken with calculated precision. Being one himself, Roth could recognize hired guns when he saw them. He had no doubt that if he so much as twitched the wrong way toward his own pistol that he would be dead inside of a second.

"So," the man in the middle of the room said. "Let's get down to the nitty gritty."

NINETEEN

Clint walked with Elena back into town. He took her straight to the spot where Eclipse was waiting and climbed onto the Darley Arabian's back. After helping her into the saddle behind him, Clint snapped the reins and got the stallion moving at a quick trot.

Working his way through town, he scanned the streets for signs of James or any men who might be on Frye's payroll. From what he'd seen already, the hired guns were the type who strutted around like angry peacocks rather than sticking to the gutters where they belonged.

Those types were always quicker to get into a fight, but were also much easier to see. Clint figured they wouldn't be back until they'd gathered up enough numbers to come at their targets in force, which would probably give him at least a few more hours of peace and quiet.

So far, it seemed as though Clint was right. Although there were the occasional threatening stares thrown his way, nobody seemed ready to jump just yet.

Elena wrapped her arms around Clint's midsection. When they'd first started riding, she seemed to still be feeling the aftereffects of their lovemaking. She nuzzled in close and pressed her body tight against his. But it

didn't take long for her to remind herself about all that
was going on and all the dangers that lurked in the growing shadows, waiting for the right moment to strike.

She couldn't see anything too well from where she was
sitting, but she could feel the tension coming off of Clint
like waves of heat pouring through his skin. Something
was wrong. She just didn't know exactly what it was.

"What's the matter, Clint?" she asked. "What's going
on?"

"Nothing."

She twisted in the saddle, trying to get a better look
around while keeping as close to Clint as possible. "Is it
Frye? Oh my god . . . is it James? There's something
wrong, I can feel it."

"Relax, Elena."

"Then why aren't we heading home?"

"I just want to take a look around to make sure things
are still the way I left them."

Although it had been less than an hour since he and
James had parted ways, Clint felt as though it had been
days since he'd seen the other man. It didn't help that part
of him was still angry that he'd allowed himself to take
time with Elena. Suddenly, Clint heard something that
snapped his attention toward the street that he'd just
passed by. Pulling on Eclipse's reins, he brought the Darley Arabian to a stop and turned him back in the other
direction.

Eclipse whinnied a bit under the sudden change, but
adjusted well enough. The stallion bobbed its head and
walked a little quicker once he felt the reins snap gently
against the back of his neck.

"Is that what I think it is?" Elena asked while straining
her back to try and look over Clint's shoulder.

"It sure looks like it."

Within seconds, Clint had ridden down the street and
was coming up alongside the wagon whose rattling wheels

had caught his attention. James sat in the driver's seat and turned to look just as Clint was pulling back on Eclipse's reins and brought his own team to a stop as well.

Not wasting a single moment, Elena dropped down from the saddle and ran over to the wagon. She hopped up onto the back of the cart and rushed over to wrap her arms around her brother's neck.

"There you are, Jim Halliwell," she said in an almost motherly tone. "I thought you'd gone off and gotten yourself killed!"

Once James had gotten over the surprise of the pair's sudden appearance, he laughed easily and set the wagon's brake with a swift kick of his right foot. He then turned and lifted Elena easily off her feet to drop her down onto the seat beside him.

"That wasn't exactly what I was aiming for when I set out," James said. "But Clint here stepped in at just the right time."

Clint shrugged and nodded toward Elena. "Actually, you should probably thank your sister for that. She's the one who told me you would probably need a helping hand. She even told me exactly where to look for you."

James looked back at his sister.

Still fussing over James's bruises, Elena rolled her eyes. "Today's the first time I was ever happy that you were such a creature of habit, big brother. I swear, I'll never make fun of your boring routines ever again."

"Did you get the rest of your supplies?" Clint asked.

James nodded while trying to brush away his sister's insistent fingers. "I sure did. Some of the shopkeepers even gave me a discount on account of what happened to Frye."

Clucking her tongue, Elena asked, "Did any of them offer to help put that son of a bitch in the ground where he belongs?"

"No," James replied. "Not exactly."

"Then to hell with 'em. We've got all the help we need."

Clint had to laugh quietly at Elena's barbed comments. Since the first time he'd met her, she'd always been a spitfire. It was good to see that some things never changed . . . no matter how many Fryes were out there doing as much damage as they could.

"We'd best get home," Clint said. "Otherwise, some of these boys watching us are going to get bad ideas in their heads."

Standing up in the wagon, Elena clenched her fists and stomped a foot. "I say let them come. That is unless they'd rather hide like—"

The rest of her threat was cut off when James reached up, took hold of her wrist and pulled her down. Although it would have seemed rough coming from anyone else, he handled her just like any other brother would handle his little sister.

"That's enough, Evie," James said as his sister's backside landed on the bench. "We're going home for some supper."

Elena seemed annoyed when she looked at her brother, but that faded as soon as the wagon lurched into motion. "Follow us, Clint," she said. "I'll make us pork chops and applesauce."

"That sounds great," Clint replied as he got Eclipse walking next to the wagon. "I've worked up one hell of an appetite."

On the bench, both James and Elena grinned at that comment. Both of them, however, were thinking about two completely different things.

TWENTY

Once he'd cooled down a bit, Frye was content to let the rest of the night slip by without getting too worked up about his problem with the Halliwells. Although he'd taken a beating that day, that was only because of the sudden arrival of this stranger who'd taken it upon himself to step in on James's behalf.

But like any good manager, Frye had delegated enough tasks to keep his men busy for the rest of the night and probably well into the morning. After they were through, those men would report in and Frye would roll his sleeves up and get back to work. Until then, however, it was time for him to sit back and enjoy being the most powerful man in Barryville.

That status came with its benefits. He had a home that was close enough to town for him to get anywhere he needed in a matter of minutes. It was also far enough away that he wasn't kept awake by the constant ruckus made by the locals. Sometimes, their whining and complaining was almost too much for him to bear. Now that he could live the way he was meant to, Frye indulged in one of the luxuries that was most precious to him: quiet.

Of course, this was only one of the luxuries that Frye

allotted himself once he'd taken his proper place at the head of that town. Another was just entering his room carrying a pitcher of steaming hot water.

Reclining in a claw-foot bath tub with a cigar clenched in his teeth, Frye leaned his head back and exhaled slowly as the water was poured in to warm up the entire bath. When he opened his eyes, he took a good look at the girl holding the pitcher.

She wasn't more than eighteen years old. Frye knew that because if she was any older than that, he would have tossed her out of his home and smacked the living hell out of the madam who'd sent her to him. But he didn't have to worry about doing anything like that tonight. This girl was perfectly suited to his tastes.

Her sandy brown hair was pulled back into a pair of pigtails, which showed off the slender curve of her neck. There was still a light dusting of freckles on her skin and as she leaned over to empty the pitcher, the steam from Frye's bath caused the thin cotton camisole she wore to cling tightly to her flesh.

Besides the camisole, the only other thing she had on was a set of bloomers, which rode down low upon her hips. She was a trim, tall girl with small, pert breasts. The little nipples poked through the material of her camisole and she seemed to be trying to cover herself up with the position of her arms.

"What's your name, girl?" Frye asked.

She looked at him with big, blue eyes, blinked once and said, "Sarah."

Frye nodded in approval and moved up so that he was sitting straight up in the tub. "Come over here, Sarah."

She took a slow step and lowered her eyes so that she wasn't staring down at his naked body. The coy act was just that; just another requirement specified by Frye when he'd put in his standing order at the town's cathouse for nights like this one.

And this girl fit his wishes to the letter. She moved slowly and sensuously, her bare feet hardly even making a sound as she padded along the floor. When he reached out for her, Sarah set the pitcher down and moved so that his hand could just make it to her smooth, slender hip.

Frye ran his fingers over her trim contours and reached out a bit more so her could feel her tight little backside for himself. The little sigh she let out when he touched her showed Frye that she was liking his attention more than she was allowed to let on. And when he looked up at her face, he saw the experienced woman peeking through from behind the innocent facade.

"Take these off," Frye said while tugging on the top of her bloomers.

She did as she was told. Slipping her fingers beneath the waist of her thin cotton leggings, Sarah moved her hands down over her hips, wriggling just enough to help them along.

"That's the way, girl," Frye urged. "Nice and slow."

Turning on the balls of her feet, Sarah moved her body in a way to expertly prolong the simple act of undressing. The thin material slid along her hips while slowly revealing the delicate curve of her bottom. Once she'd positioned herself so that Frye was given the best view possible, she bent slightly at the waist and continued to peel away the leggings.

Her buttocks were slender and tight, with just enough of a curve to make them pleasing to the eye. Her skin was flawless and creamy, giving off the faint odor of lilacs and her own natural sweetness. When the bloomers were finally down to her knees, the girl bent down even further while shifting her hips from side to side.

It took every bit of self-control he had for Frye to keep himself from reaching out and pulling her into the tub with him right then. He managed somehow to hold back a little, but leaned in close enough to her so he could move the palm of one hand over the smooth curve of her ass and slide his fingers between her legs.

Although she looked back at him with that innocent look in her eyes, Sarah couldn't stop herself from moaning softly when Frye's fingers grazed the lips of her pussy. She spread her legs open just enough for him to rub the sweet spot between her thighs, placing her hands on her knees while arching her back.

Suddenly, Frye pulled his hand back and leaned against the side of the tub. The moment his hands were off of her, Sarah straightened up and turned around. The hair between her legs was the same creamy brown as the hair on her head. It looked like fine down or even silk.

Sarah leaned forward and put her hands on the top of the tub. "I'm cold." She pouted in a way that made Frye even stiffer beneath the level of the water. "Can I come in there with you?"

Holding up a hand, he answered, "You were reading my mind, girl."

Taking his hand, Sarah lifted one leg up and into the tub, waiting for a moment so that Frye could get a nice look at the soft tuft between her thighs. She then stepped all the way into the water, turned so that her back was to him and settled with her shoulders against his chest.

"Mmmm," Sarah purred. "That's better."

Frye smiled and moved his wet hands over her breasts, peeling the soaked camisole off her body.

Some folks said he had blood on his hands after climbing to the top of the food chain in Barryville and Frye seldom denied it. Times like these, however, made it all worth it.

TWENTY-ONE

Roth did his best to ignore all the ways he could get hurt or killed in that fancy hotel suite. If he said one word out of turn or took one wrong step, he might get gunned down by any of the hired killers positioned about the room. Or, he might just get beaten to death by the hulking monster named Bullock who'd answered the door.

Although these were all definitely concerns in his mind, Roth pushed them aside. After all, he was used to putting his life on the line in the name of cutting a good deal. That was what Frye had been paying him to do for years.

"You want to get to business?" Roth asked in his toughest voice. "Then let's do it. I'd prefer to get out of this place as soon as I can."

The fat man in the tailored suit grinned. He was seemingly unaffected by anything Roth might say or do. Lyle Evans instead got to his feet and walked up to Roth until he was practically nose to nose with the other man. "I didn't get to where I am from giving a damn about what comes out of the mouths of pissants like you. So save me your strutting and say what's on your mind." When he stepped back, some of the amiability that had been there before seeped back into his features. "Care for a drink?"

Despite all the physical threats in the room, Roth was somehow more shaken by what Evans had just said. Feeling shaken was one thing. Looking it was something altogether different. "Sure, I'll take a drink. Whiskey if you've got it."

Without taking his eyes from Roth, Evans snapped his fingers. One of the gunmen behind him moved toward the small bar near the back of the room and started fixing two glasses.

"What's on your mind?" Evans asked.

Taking the drink that was held out to him by one of the nameless killers, Roth took a sip and let the expensive liquor trickle down his throat. "There's a new player in town, that's what."

"You mean Adams?"

This time, Roth was unable to keep the surprise from showing on his face.

Nodding, Evans said, "Yeah . . . I know about him. He didn't seem to have any trouble making you and your bunch look like fools."

"They're not my bunch. Frye's still giving the orders, which is why Adams isn't dead already."

"Oh, is that so?"

"Yes, sir, it is."

"And do you know anything about Clint Adams?"

Roth didn't reply. He just took another sip of whiskey and let his eyes burn with the anger that had been building up inside of him.

"Adams isn't the kind of man you just gun down in the street," Evans continued. "Plenty of others have tried and if they walked away from the encounter, they decided to hang up their guns."

"And what makes you such an expert?"

"I hear things." Turning his back on Roth, Evans walked over to a window and peered through the glass. "Granted, some of the stories may be overly exaggerated, but they can't all be lies. Some of my own men have seen Adams at work. I've even seen him myself." Evans wheeled around to fix his eyes upon his visitor. "It was quite a show, what happened earlier."

"I've already explained myself to Frye—"

"And I don't expect an explanation from you. Frankly, I don't need one. Even a blind man could tell that he caught you boys with your pants around your ankles and sent you packing with blood in your mouths and egg on your faces. Like I said . . . quite a show."

Roth had something to say, but he held his tongue when he noticed that he was being closely watched by all those other physical threats he'd spotted earlier. Instead, he washed away his threats with another pull from the whiskey.

Evans turned back around to look through the window. "But that doesn't change anything. Adams is just another unforeseen obstacle. Nothing more."

"So our deal is still on?"

"Yes . . . but I've been forced to change its structure in order to surmount this newest obstacle."

Roth didn't like the sound of that, which was obvious in the narrowing of his eyes and the scowl that eased across his features. "What do you mean, you're changing it?"

"In essence, it's still the same. You still get to lead your boss down my employer's path, right up to the point where Frye winds up another casualty in this little local feud. Only, with Adams in the picture, that just means that we have to step up the timetable and raise the stakes a bit.

"Since Mister Halliwell will no doubt be heading out for that ranch pretty soon, I'll need you to make sure that his entire family goes with him. And Adams as well. They all die tonight."

"What?" Roth asked. "Why?"

"Those, my good man, are two questions that you don't need to ask. Not now . . . and not ever."

Roth's anger flared within his chest and caused him to surge forward with his fist clenched almost tight enough to shatter the glass in his hand. "I may take money from you, but nobody talks to me like—"

He made all of one and a half steps of progress before feeling something similar to a vice being clamped onto his shoulder. Roth took a quick look to see Bullock staring down at him with enough intensity to melt the bad intentions right out of him.

"No need to get yourself all worked up," Evans said. "What I have in mind shouldn't be too difficult. Even for someone like you."

That last comment was meant to test Roth's self-control. Even though he knew that fact, Roth still had to fight to keep his temper in check. It was a struggle, but he managed to do well enough for Bullock to ease up a little.

"Fine," Roth said in a strained voice. "Just remember that I get paid more for any killing my men do."

"Of course. Just try to get the job done this time."

TWENTY-TWO

Even though the water inside Frye's tub had turned luke-warm several minutes ago, he didn't seem to notice the temperature change in the slightest. That was mainly due to the fact that he had Sarah in there with him to keep every part of him warm.

He leaned his back against the side of the tub, his head resting on the tapered edge. Sitting in his lap and positioned so that she was facing him, Sarah worked the palms of her hands over his chest and shoulders, rubbing in a lotion with a vague, flowery scent.

Normally, Frye didn't like the perfumed concoction, but this time he couldn't bring himself to complain. Especially since the girl rubbing it into his skin was riding slowly up and down upon his erect penis.

Frye let out a slow, satisfied breath as Sarah came down one more time. Her pussy was tight and contracting around his column of flesh in a massage that sent ripples of ecstasy up and down through his body. The little nipples at the tips of her pert breasts were stiff, pink nubs, dripping with bath water, which he periodically dripped over her skin.

Although sopping wet, her hair was still pulled into

pigtails, which stuck to the bare skin of her shoulders. As she tended to him, Sarah followed her own hands with her eyes, drinking in the sight without saying a single word.

Suddenly, Frye felt the thin pink lips between her legs clench around him. That sent a pulse of pleasure through him so quick and intense that it made him lose all the control he'd been practicing up to that moment. He reached down below the level of the water and grabbed hold of her buttocks, thrusting his hips upward to drive himself all the way inside Sarah's body.

The girl leaned forward and grabbed hold of the sides of the tub, moaning softly in response.

"You like that?" he whispered.

When she didn't answer right away, Frye grabbed her tighter and pumped into her again. "I asked if you liked that!"

Since she'd been with Frye before, Sarah was used to the way he talked to her. Most of the other girls were uncomfortable with him, but she had to admit that she liked the rough way he had about him. Sometimes, she even found herself wanting to be with him when she was sharing her bed with another of her regular customers.

Maybe it was the power the man had. Or maybe it was just the way he took control of her and did whatever he wanted, making her feel like she was out of control rather than leading him by the nose the way she would any other man.

Whatever her reasons, Sarah was hard-pressed to think about them much at the moment. All that was going through her mind was the way Frye snarled at her and the way his cock pumped up into her harder and harder when she didn't answer his question right away.

After she'd let him thrust between her legs one more time, Sarah closed her eyes and lowered herself so that her breasts brushed up against Frye's chest. "Yes," she groaned. "Yes, I like it."

"I know what you like even more," he answered. And with that, he pulled out of her and pushed her away while backing himself as far against the tub as he could. "Turn around."

Sarah turned her face so that he wouldn't see just how much she'd been anticipating those words. Instead, she got to her knees and maneuvered within the tight confines of the bathtub as best she could. When she had her back to him, she crawled forward so that she was bent over the opposite edge of the tub with her upper body hanging slightly out.

Frye watched all of this intently. He savored every slow movement and the way she maintained her innocent appearance even while presenting him with a perfect view of her backside and spread legs. She arched her back and peeked over her shoulder. It was those wide eyes that made her look so innocent. Sarah could be doing anything at all, but those eyes would still make her look like something clean and untouched.

Those eyes were what allowed her to charge more than any other girl in Barryville's cathouse.

Moving in behind her, Frye reached forward to run his hands up along her sides. She writhed in between his palms like a cat while making a soft, satisfied moan in the back of her throat. He slid his hands further along her skin until he could cup her firm breasts. His hands fully covered her slender curves and when he rubbed the hard nipples, she groaned a little louder.

Frye's penis was pressed up tight against her backside. As she moved her hips back and forth against him, his need to be inside her again almost became too much to bear. Taking hold of her hips, he fit the tip of his cock between her legs and slipped it into her tight, moist little pussy.

Although she looked like a girl, Sarah moaned like the woman she was when she felt him pound into her from behind. Those moans became even louder when Frye took hold of her pigtails in one hand and pulled back her head just enough to draw her hair taut.

Using his other hand to rub along her buttocks and breasts, Frye thrust into her again and again, pounding Sarah until she cried out loud.

"God," she moaned. "Don't stop."

The water inside the bathtub splashed up over the edge and onto the floor. The sound it made blended in with the sound of Frye's hand slapping against the side of Sarah's buttocks. He knew she liked that every bit as much as he liked doing it, so he slapped her one more time just hard enough to make her squeal with delight.

As the explosion built up within him, Frye held onto Sarah's waist and pulled her body closer to his own so he could pump into her even deeper. Sarah seemed to miss the hair pulling, but she was quickly swept up in the steady rhythm of Frye's cock gliding between her legs. She arched her back, held onto the tub and enjoyed the sensation until both of their pleasure had run its course.

When he pulled out, Frye leaned back against the side of the tub and watched as Sarah climbed up out of the water. Droplets of moisture clung to her trim curves, running over her smooth little breasts and down along her flat stomach.

She took her time fetching her clothes, pulling on her camisole first and sliding it down onto her body. Even though it was the reverse of a striptease, the way Sarah wriggled into her bloomers was enough to get Frye ready for a repeat performance.

Just as he was about to call her over again, Frye's train of thought was derailed by a sudden loud rapping upon his door.

"Goddammit," he hissed under his breath.

Looking from the door to Frye, Sarah stood next to the tub with her black lacy dress in her hands. Her underclothes stuck to her wet skin, showing off every detail of her body almost better than if she'd simply taken everything off again. She knew that Frye might want to take her again, so she waited before putting the dress back on.

Although Frye's first impulse had been to find out who was knocking at his door, his priorities started to change the more he drank in the sight of Sarah standing before him. There was something about the slender girl that made him want to lock himself in a room with her and let the rest of the world pass him by.

The knock came again. This time, it was followed by a muffled voice from the other side of the door.

"Open the door, Zeke," it said. "We've got problems. Clint Adams is staying on with the Halliwells."

Once again, Frye's priorities shifted. Standing up in the tub, he looked at Sarah and pointed toward the door. "Let him in and get out."

TWENTY-THREE

Frye was still buttoning up his shirt when Michael Roth came into his room. The gunman held open the door and watched as Sarah walked past him and left. Roth made no attempt to hide the way he watched the young woman as she strode away.

"I love watching that one go," Roth said.

Stepping forward, Frye reached out with one hand and slapped the other man across the head. "Get your eyes off of her and pay attention. If you don't justify your presence here, I'm liable to start getting real upset. I could be doing a lot better things than standing here and talking to you."

"Yeah, I bet." After taking one last look at Sarah's behind, Roth shut the door and threw the latch into place.

"Now, what's this you're saying about Adams and Halliwell?" Frye asked.

"Just like I told you. It looks like Adams is going to stick around for a bit and help Jim take that ranch away from us."

"Adams is still with him?"

"Yep. And it doesn't look like he's set to leave anytime soon."

"That's unfortunate." Frye's tone was solemn and colder than ice.

"But there's no reason to worry. I've got it all under control."

Judging by the way he looked at Roth, Frye believed that last statement about as much as he believed in the Ghost of Christmas Past. "*You* . . . have it under control?"

"That's what I said, isn't it?"

"So how about you share this wonderful plan of yours with me before I die from anticipation?"

"Nothing to it, really," Roth said. "Me and some of the boys go over to the Halliwell place and fill it full of lead. Adams might have taken us by surprise before, but now that we know what we're dealing with it shouldn't be that big of a job."

"You do know who Clint Adams is, right?"

"Yeah. So the man can shoot. Is that supposed to scare us? We just won't give him a chance to impress anyone with any fancy gunslinging. Besides, I plan on giving him a lot more to think about than just protecting one man."

"Is that a fact, now? And what else might Adams be thinking about once the lead starts to fly?"

"Protecting the entire family, of course. Spread any man too thin and he's bound to make a mistake somewhere along the line. Even a piece of work like Clint Adams."

Frye thought it over for a minute or so and then started to nod. Even with his rumpled shirt hanging out at odd angles and the tussled mess of hair upon his head, he still managed to look like the boss. His eyes maintained their proud glint and his bearing remained straight and commanding.

"How many of the boys do you need for this, do you think?" Frye asked.

"All of them. Well . . . all of them who can still get along all right after what happened before."

"There's just some bumps and bruises," Frye said dismissively. "There shouldn't be any shortage of volunteers. Especially when they hear that they'll be going after Adams for a measure of payback."

"That's what I figure."

Rubbing his chin as though he was still contemplating his decision, Frye was thinking about something else entirely. Mainly, he didn't like the way Roth was taking the initiative all of a sudden regarding such important business decisions. Normally, the gunman had been nothing but muscle. But now he was starting to come up with plans and plotting major moves on his own.

What made Frye even more nervous was the distinct possibility that Roth wasn't making these decisions at all. Although that was much more likely, that sat in Frye's gut like a piece of rotten beef.

"So you and the rest go in shooting?" Frye asked. "That's your big plan?"

"You always said that simple things work better."

"Yes, I did. Fine, then. Take as many of the boys as you can scrounge up. I'll send Cobb to round up the rest and tell them all to take orders from you as if they'd heard them from my own mouth."

Roth could feel the victorious smirk tugging at the corners of his mouth. Those words had been exactly what he'd been waiting for. And now that he'd gotten Frye to say them, the rest of his plan seemed suddenly well within his reach.

"When you see Cobb on your way out," Frye said, "tell him to come in here. You know where to find the others."

Roth nodded and turned to leave. He stopped when he heard Frye noisily clearing his throat.

"One last thing," Frye said once he knew he'd gotten Roth's attention again. "Where have you been since we've last talked?"

"Getting a drink. Checking up on a few things. Why?"

"You haven't been back to that suite at the Hilltop Lodge, have you?"

After so many years of playing poker, Roth's card face had been nearly perfected. Without so much as a twitch, he shrugged and shook his head. "No."

TWENTY-FOUR

It didn't take long for Clint to get anxious as he rode alongside James's wagon. The Halliwells lived in a cottage just outside of town, but they were moving so slowly that it felt as though they were still hours away from their destination. Clint could have gotten there a hell of a lot faster if he touched his spurs to Eclipse's sides and hung on to the reins, but then he would have left the wagon alone. And since he was more concerned with keeping Elena and her brother safe, he kept pace with the wagon, which was going as fast as James's old nag could pull it.

Clint used the time he had to think over everything that had happened since he'd gotten into Barryville. Although things seemed pretty straightforward on the surface, there were more things bothering him about James's situation the more Clint thought it over. He figured he could get some answers once everyone was safe inside their own home, so it would be best to just keep an eye out while they rode and wait until then.

The town itself had just melted into the background as James's wagon rattled along the trail leading toward the less populated outskirts. Stretched out before them was a thick array of trees and rocky terrain, dotted with the oc-

casional home that had been built upon its own tract of
land.

Each of the homes was flickering with firelight ema-
nating from within, making the outside air seem that much
colder in comparison. Just when Clint felt closer to finally
reaching the house, he saw James pull back on his reins
and bring his wagon to a stop.

"What's the matter?" Clint asked. "Why'd you stop?"

James cocked his head and stared into the distance
ahead of him. "Look there," he replied.

Clint looked and saw nothing at first. Then, as his eyes
got more adjusted to the dark mixture of shadows and
shapes camouflaged within the night hues, he picked out
the single shape that had caught James's attention. By the
looks of it, there was a single figure waiting in the middle
of the road about thirty yards away from the Halliwells'
front door.

Looking over to Elena, Clint asked, "Is that someone
waiting for you?"

Elena had been in good spirits throughout the entire
ride. When she peered ahead into the gloomy darkness,
the smile melted off her face and she pressed herself
tighter against the wagon's seat. "That's someone waiting
for us, but I don't know who it is."

"What about your brother or mother?"

"Mother doesn't leave the house after sundown and the
only way that could be my brother was if he grew another
three or four inches since this morning."

"Then that means it's someone else who wants to talk
to us. After everything I've seen and heard, I doubt that's
a very good thing."

James reached around behind him and pulled out a long
double-barrel shotgun. "I'm with Clint," he said. "Evie . . .
stay here while me and him check this out."

"I will *not* just sit by and wait while—"

"Evie," James interrupted. "Stay here."

After hearing that tone in her brother's voice, Elena lost all of her resolve to defy him. She crossed her arms over her chest, looking very much like the little sister, and dropped all the way back into her seat. James glared at her for a moment until he was satisfied that she was actually going to listen to him for a change. He then checked to make sure the shotgun was loaded and cocked back both of its hammers.

"This might be bad, Clint," James said. "You don't have to do anything if you don't want to."

"I appreciate the thought, but I'm already far enough in this already. Getting out now would just be stupid."

That wasn't much of a reason, but it was enough for James. Especially when he saw that, not only was the figure carrying a rifle, but it was also not alone.

As Clint rode Eclipse farther up the path, he saw other figures stepping out from the shadows surrounding the Halliwell cottage. There were also a few more coming from the line of nearby trees as well as some others walking up behind the wagon.

It was hard to say exactly how many there were. All Clint knew was that there were enough to present a problem. After all, it didn't take an expert marksman to kill a man in a crossfire.

"Clint," James whispered as he jumped down from the wagon and jogged up next to Eclipse. "Do you hear that?"

Even before James had asked that question, Clint was starting to hear voices coming from within the cottage. They were definitely voices raised in some kind of argument or alarm. One was definitely female.

"There's more of them inside the house," James said. "Whoever they are, my brother and mother are in there with them."

TWENTY-FIVE

Clint swung down from the saddle just as James was starting to move toward the cottage. Placing a firm hand on
James's shoulder, Clint stopped the other man before he
could get too far. When James swung around to glare at
Clint, he looked as though he was about to take a swing
out of sheer reflex.

"Don't be stupid," Clint warned. "Now's not the time."

After taking a moment to collect himself, James nodded
and said, "Yeah, you're right. But we've got to do something."

"Don't worry about that. We're definitely going to do
something. Just come with me and follow my lead."

That seemed to be enough to calm James down for the
moment and he waited for Clint to start heading down the
path before falling into step beside him. His fingers tightened around the shotgun, but he kept the weapon aiming
toward the ground.

Stopping about ten yards from the man who was standing in the middle of the trail, Clint took another look
around to make sure he wasn't about to be taken by surprise. The wagon was sitting in a wide open space and
anyone trying to sneak up on it would have to cover a

fair amount of ground before they could get there. From
what he could tell, the others were either showing themselves to strengthen the first man's position or holding
back for now.

"What's your business here?" Clint asked.

The man looked vaguely familiar to Clint, but he
couldn't think of a name to go with the face. He had an
average build and was dressed like all the other men
who'd been in town when Clint had found James.

"My business ain't none of your concern, Adams," the
man said. "So why don't you just get back on that horse
of yours and ride away?"

Clint took a closer look at the man. "I remember you
now. I recognize that big knot on your head. Last time I
heard your voice, you were about to cry like an old
woman after I put you down with that axe handle."

That comment most definitely had the desired effect on
the younger man. Listening to Clint speak was almost
enough to break down his resolve and cause him to charge
forward like an angry bull.

Taking full advantage of the reaction he'd caused, Clint
nodded slowly and locked eyes with him. "You want my
advice? Round up all your friends and leave because
you're sitting in at a game with stakes higher than you
can afford."

James leaned closer to Clint and whispered so that none
of the others could hear. "How did he know who you
are?"

"Doesn't matter," Clint said with a shrug. "What does
matter is what's going on inside that house."

James took a look for himself, squinting so that he
could make out more of how the shapes were moving
behind his cottage's windows. Where the shadows were
moving around and making noise before, now they were
quietly standing in place. Only a couple slivers of shapes
could be seen, but it was obvious that they were peeking

through the edges of the curtains at what was going on outside.

"As long as they're watching us," Clint explained, "that means they're not doing anything else to whoever's in there."

Although that gave James some degree of comfort, he still wasn't sure if he could be completely happy about drawing the full attention of at least half a dozen armed men. His heart thumped in his chest and he did his best to keep his reservations from showing on his face.

"That one there is Cobb," James said while nodding toward the only gunman who'd done any talking so far.

Clint made sure that the wagon was still clear before facing Cobb and saying, "So you are all here. You're all real good at scaring women and children. What do you want?"

Cobb waited until some of the others had drifted out from the shadows to stand around him. Once he could see the other hired guns standing nearby, he said, "Mister Frye wants the deed to that ranch. He also wants the deed to this property here."

"Now wait a minute!" James snarled as he instinctively began to rush toward Cobb.

Once again, Clint stopped him with a hand on his shoulder. "Why do you want this property? And what the hell is so special about that damn ranch? Is this just a matter of pride for a couple rich men with nothing else better to do?"

Cobb smiled. "A matter of pride? Yeah . . . you might call it that. Everyone in town knows better than to go against what Mister Frye wants, 'cause if they do they got to pay the price. If'n he lets a farmer like this one spit in his face too many times, he needs to teach him a lesson."

"I don't understand," Clint said. "If Frye wants this family out of the way, why not just let them pack up and head west? Wouldn't that solve all your boss's problems, or would that not allow him to settle his little issue with pride?"

Cobb seemed to be stumped by that one. Rather than try to figure it out, however, he opted for the shorter route. "Shut yer mouth, Adams," he shouted. "I said this don't concern you!"

"That's where you're wrong." Clint's tone had changed from conversational to deadly in the space of a second. "It concerns me since I've decided not to let you hurt this man or his family. And you'll only have your boss to blame if the one getting hurt turns out to be you."

Shifting his eyes toward James, Cobb stuck out a finger and added, "You brought this on yourself, Halliwell. All you needed to do was step aside at the very beginning and none of this would'a happened. Now, we got to hurt you, take your house and property and hurt that nice little family of yours."

When Clint heard that, he cursed under his breath since he knew what was going to happen next. Sure enough, James lifted his shotgun and pulled free of Clint's restraining hand. The moment the rest of those gunmen saw what James was doing, they all burst into motion themselves.

Once that had happened, Clint knew there was no other option left but to jump into the fray and hope for the best.

TWENTY-SIX

Sometimes, Clint found that he could talk his way out of a fight. Not that he was afraid of Cobb, Frye or any of the other men. Far from it. But the way he saw it, getting those gunmen to walk away would have been a hell of a lot easier than taking them on while also having to worry about James or the rest of his family catching a bullet.

As attractive as that option might have seemed, it flew out the window faster than a panicked canary when James lifted his shotgun and started to charge toward Cobb. Before James could even cover five feet worth of ground, the other men's guns had cleared leather and the sound of hammers cocking filled the air.

Clint's senses snapped into a faster speed that had been developed after years of surviving when the lead started to fly. It wasn't anything more than finely honed reflexes that allowed him to take a breath and see what was going on as though the rest of the world had shifted to a slower pace.

He used those senses to pick out his first target, looking for the gunman who seemed to be the biggest threat coming out of the gate. The one who caught his eye first was a gunman to Cobb's left who didn't seem as eager as all

the others. That one sighted down the barrel of his pistol
and was about to squeeze off a shot that might have
caught James directly in the chest.

The only thing keeping that from happening was the
speed of Clint's own hand as he plucked the modified Colt
from his holster and drew a bead on his target. His moves
were completely natural and he aimed as though he was
simply pointing his finger at where he wanted the bullet
to go. When he squeezed the trigger, the Colt bucked once
in Clint's hand and sent a piece of hot lead roaring
through the air.

Still concentrating on James, the gunman didn't look in
Clint's direction until it was too late. Attracted by the
sound of gunfire, his eyes snapped over to the puff of
smoke coming from the Colt as a sudden burning pain
chewed through his shoulder.

Clint's bullet tore a path through bone and muscle,
forcing the gunman to lower his weapon as his arm dan-
gled limply from his shoulder. It had all happened so
quickly that his finger still tensed around the trigger, firing
off the bullet that had been intended for James into the
ground next to his feet.

Having taken his shot and kept James alive, at least for
another few seconds, Clint searched out his next target
right as James closed the gap between himself and Cobb.

Unlike Frye's killers, James's first impulse was not to
kill the other man. Instead, he gripped the shotgun with
both hands, pulled it back like a battering ram and sent
the end of the barrel straight into Cobb's gut.

The impact came just as Cobb had drawn his pistol and
was about to take his shot. Reeling from the dull pain and
finding himself suddenly unable to draw a breath, the gunman let out a wheezing groan as his eyes became wide as
saucers.

"You son of a bitch," James snarled. "Nobody threatens
my family like that. Nobody!" And with that last word,

he pulled back the shotgun as if to take another swing.
He came up short, however, when another one of the gunmen grabbed hold of the shotgun's stock and tried to yank
it from James's hands.

Clint was already moving at a quick jog, twisting and
ducking to make himself a more difficult target for the
men who'd now taken it upon themselves to put him
down. There were three more standing around Cobb. Two
of them were moving in closer to intercept Clint while
the other was stepping back so he could take better aim.

Even as he charged straight into the midst of those first
two, Clint was more concerned with the third. After all,
he knew firsthand that trying to make a killing shot when
close enough to punch your target boiled down to a lot
of dumb luck and near misses.

Shooting a man while he was being held by two others
usually took a lot of guesswork out of the equation.

Since James seemed to be holding his own with Cobb,
Clint let those two go for the moment. The rest of the
gunmen had set their sights upon him anyway, since they
were all probably itching to be the one who put the Gunsmith on the ground.

As the two closest gunmen converged on his position,
Clint did the last thing they were expecting and didn't
stop moving after they'd blocked his way. Instead, he
twisted his right arm back and then used his waist to
gather up some more momentum as he swung that same
forearm out in a straight line. The blow connected with
one of the gunmen's chest and knocked him clean off his
feet. Letting out a pained grunt, that one hit the ground
on his back and rolled onto his side.

Clint kept right on moving toward the house, but didn't
forget about the other two he'd have to get through along
the way. The closest of those rushed Clint from behind in
an attempt to smash the butt of his pistol against the back
of Clint's neck.

Pretending to leave himself open for the attempted bushwhacking, Clint waited until the last moment before stepping to the side and spinning in a tight circle. When he came to a stop, he was standing to the attacker's left and was in perfect position to bring his knee up and catch the other man in the lower abdomen.

Clint could hear the gunman straining to draw a breath. Just as he was about to push past that one, however, Clint spotted the third gunman who'd moved away from the scuffle in order to get himself a better line of fire. As Clint's eyes focused on that man, he was just in time to find himself staring down the barrel of a gun.

Next, there came a puff of dark smoke and a shower of sparks as the hammer dropped.

Clint let his reflexes take over and tried to get out of the incoming bullet's path before it dug a tunnel through his own body. He pitched himself to the side and away from the other gunmen, his body turning in a quick, tight spiral.

The world spun crazily around him and soon the ground was coming up to smack Clint squarely on the chin. A split second before impact, he managed to get both hands beneath him, which prevented him from getting an unhealthy taste of dirt. It wasn't the most graceful of maneuvers, but it was enough to save his life. Of course, it had also forced him to drop his gun.

He wasn't the only one to notice that, however. Grinning widely, the third gunman thumbed back his hammer and squeezed off another shot toward a spot directly between Clint's eyes.

TWENTY-SEVEN

Clint saw the gun aiming at him for less than a second before he was once again in motion. This time, rather than keep his chin off the ground, he pressed the side of his face directly into it while rolling toward the incoming fire.

The shot blasted through the air and hissed over his head like an angry hornet. If Clint was hit, he wouldn't have known until a time when he could allow himself to think about such things. Just then, the only thing he concerned himself with was to keep moving.

Keep rolling forward.

Keep hoping that he'd done enough to cheat death one more time.

He came to a stop by thrusting out one foot, which slapped against the ground. Not only had Clint wound up looking straight up at the gunman who was no more than five yards away, but he was also only a few inches away from his Colt, which he'd been forced to drop during his fall.

Clint's hand was a blur of motion as he reached out to grab the Colt, take quick aim and pull the trigger. The pistol barked loudly and spat its fiery payload into the air. Whipping through the air, the single round closed the distance between Clint and the gunman in the blink of an eye, punching a messy hole through the other man's chest.

Gasping once in painful surprise, the gunman blinked disbelievingly, dropped to his knees and fell facefirst into the dirt.

Clint could hear sounds of struggle all around. They came from the house as well as behind him, letting him know that all hell had indeed broken loose. Glancing over his shoulder to check on the wagon, Clint spotted a figure rushing toward him.

Wearing a mask of grim determination and pumping his legs desperately, the gunman who Clint had knocked down was making one last charge while pulling his trigger as quickly as his finger could manage. His first shot might have made it if he'd taken his time to do it right. Instead, the quick jerking motion of his finger pulled his gun low and to the side, sending the first bullet into the ground a couple feet from where Clint was laying.

The shooter had enough time to fire once more and since he saw that the next shot was going to be even less accurate than the first, Clint let him fire again.

Sure enough, the next shot didn't even come close and Clint didn't even flinch while he took aim and fired.

Clint's round found its mark in the gunman's right eye, drilling all the way through to emerge out the back of his skull. The gunman teetered on his feet for a few seconds before toppling over. He was dead before he hit the ground, learning the hard way why shooters were taught to squeeze their triggers rather than pull.

Nearby, James was locked in a struggle of his own. He was still trying to beat down Cobb while another of Frye's men dropped the handle of his gun down between James's shoulders. The blow landed with a sickening *thud,* but James didn't even seem to notice. Instead, all he could see was Cobb and all he could hear was the last threats that had been made against his kin.

Although he wasn't a match for the gunmen's skill with firearms, James was running on pure adrenaline, which had been enough to get him this far. His muscles strained while the others tried to either hold him back or push him away. His vision was red with fury and he knew that if he didn't fight now, he might not live to see tomorrow.

James took one last swing at Cobb, his knuckles landing on the side of his jaw. Since his fists were still wrapped around the shotgun, his blows packed a bigger wallop than normal and rocked the gunman wherever they landed.

Cobb took that shot and staggered back with blood streaming down his face. He wiped some away and spat the rest at James. "Get a hold of him," he said, not caring about whatever else was going on around him.

Hearing that, James wheeled around and saw the other gunman snapping back the pistol's hammer. Up until this moment, he'd managed to keep the men busy enough that they couldn't get a shot in edgewise. Now, one of the shooters had taken a moment and that was all he needed to get his weapon ready.

The other shooter reached out with his free hand to take hold of James's shotgun. He clamped his fingers around the barrel between James's hands and tried to pull the weapon free.

James still had his eyes on the other man's pistol when he felt his own weapon almost get taken from him. Knowing damn well that that shotgun had kept him alive this long, James twisted his hands in a circular motion, wrenching the shotgun out of the gunman's grip. From there, he pointed the barrel toward the gunman and pulled one of the triggers.

A blast of hot thunder roared through the air, filling the wind with stinging sparks and all but wiping out all three men's hearing.

Reflexively, one of the gunmen jumped away from the

group, leaving Cobb and James alone while patting himself down with one hand to see if all his parts were still attached and in working order.

Having never fired that shotgun at anything bigger than a possum, James turned around to face the man closest to him. Cobb was trying to say something, but the ringing in James's ears was too loud to make any of it out. What he did understand was the way Cobb snarled angrily at him while lifting his pistol up to fire.

James saw the barrel coming his way. He saw the cold, dull metal lining up until the end of the barrel stared back at him like the reaper's unblinking eye.

In that moment, he knew he only had two choices: kill or die.

Before he realized what he was doing, James's reflexes had made the decision for him and his finger clenched around the shotgun's second trigger.

Once again, the familiar roar echoed through the night. The fire erupting from the shotgun engulfed Cobb's midsection, tearing out a piece of his rib cage along with one of his lungs.

All Cobb could feel was an intense heat followed by complete numbness. His own reflexes were working as well, however, and that was how he managed to take a shot of his own before dropping into a heap on the ground.

At first, James thought he'd somehow managed to keep himself from catching any lead. Then, as the pain began to rip through him, he could feel something hot and damp soaking into his shirt. When he tried to shift the shotgun to hold it in one hand, he felt pain raking all down his spine, intensifying somewhere on his right side.

He couldn't move that arm and the empty shotgun fell heavily into the dirt.

"Jesus." He sighed as he started to feel consciousness slipping out of his grasp.

Suddenly, the door to the cottage flew open and foot-steps rushed out like a stampede. Somehow, James found himself listening to those steps and he knew that they were hitting too many wooden planks to be coming out the front. The large porch was in the back. He knew that because he'd been the one who'd built it.

Cobb stared up at him with a dead man's eyes. It was then that James spotted the other bodies laying scattered on the ground like discarded playthings. The air reeked of gunsmoke and the shrill ringing still filled his ears.

As his vision started to cloud over, he could see Clint had been the one to pull open the door and was charging in amid a hail of gunfire.

James knew he should be there at Clint's side. After all, this was his home and it was his duty to defend it. But he couldn't even keep his head up any more and all the sounds of the world boiled down to an angel's voice calling his name.

TWENTY-EIGHT

"James?"

The words drifted like leaves fluttering down to a forest floor.

"James? Do you hear me?"

After no small amount of effort, James opened his eyes and started to get up.

"No, James," the angelic voice said. "Don't try to move. Are you in any pain?"

When James blinked and took a breath, he finally started to see something through the fog. The first thing that caught his attention was the fact that he wasn't in the great beyond, but inside his own home. And the voice that had been addressing him belonged to his sister.

"Evie?" he asked.

Looking down on him with a growing smile, Elena nodded and said, "Yes, James. It's me."

"I thought . . . you were an angel."

Elena let out a sigh of relief when she heard her brother's voice. She ran a cold washcloth over his face and shook her head. "I'm not an angel, but you came awful close to meeting one."

"Don't talk like that," came another familiar voice.

"That you, Mother?"

"That's right, Jimmy."

Once again, James tried to move. And once again, he was gently forced back down. The bed creaked beneath his weight, but the mattress felt so good against his tired body. "What happened?"

Stepping forward from where he'd been standing just outside of James's field of vision, Clint made his presence known and put a comforting hand on the wounded man's left arm. "We gave Frye's boys another beating is what happened. Only you got yourself injured in the bargain."

"If we took some of those bastards with us," James said, "then it was worth every bit."

Clint's face darkened somewhat, but he nodded and put on a smile for the wounded man's benefit. "We took some of them, James. Cobb and a few of the others didn't make it."

Mother Halliwell was gnawing on a corncob pipe as she waddled over to set a bowl of hot soup next to her son's bedside. "Hope they roast in hell," she muttered. "I've been saying for God knows how long that James should burn that damn deed. It ain't nothing but trouble."

James winced as he tried to sit up, but fought whenever his sister tried to keep him on his back. Finally, he managed to get himself upright and felt as though he'd expended enough effort to run from the cottage into town and back several times. "I know, Ma. I know." He sighed. "Damn, I'm tired."

"I'll bet you are," Clint said. "You got hit pretty bad and lost a lot of blood. I thought I was carrying a corpse when I hauled you inside once all of Frye's boys cleared out of here."

"They're gone?" James asked.

It was his mother who replied. "They took off like rats with their tails on fire soon as they saw you two through the window. Them ones who were in here with me an' yer sister talked tough to a couple of women folk, but I never saw someone run faster than when they lit on out through the back door."

James looked to Clint as though he couldn't believe what he'd just heard.

Nodding, Clint said, "She's right. I checked over this place myself and I couldn't find another one anywhere near here. They must have left during the fight. The rest of them that were outside didn't stick around much longer themselves."

For a moment, James seemed to be comforted by that news. Then, his eyes snapped open again and he began looking nervously around the room. "Where's Eddie?"

"Your little brother is fine as well," Mother Halliwell said.

"Did any of those men try to hurt him?"

"He got tied up next to me, but other than that he was just shaken up. I put him in charge of making sure we're all nice and safe in here."

James found the small boy working busily with a hammer and nails fixing boards across the windows. By the looks of it, his little brother had been working diligently for some time since all but one of the windows were boarded up tight.

Finally, James sat back and sunk deeper into the sheets. "What the hell has gotten into Frye? Has he lost his damn mind?"

"I was about to ask you the same thing," Clint said.

Elena moved so that she was standing between Clint and her big brother. "Let him rest. He doesn't need to—"

"It's all right, Evie," James said. "Let the man talk."

Although he respected Elena's protectiveness, Clint knew that since the feud had turned bloody, Frye wouldn't wait much longer before striking again. He gently moved Elena aside and pulled up a chair next to James's bed.

"This has gone much further than it should have," Clint stated. "Either you're not telling me everything you know about that ranch or you don't know all there is to know, because there's got to be more to it than a rich man's fancy. Even someone like Peyton Lowry wouldn't go through this much trouble to acquire a property just because he liked the view."

Silence filled the room for the next several seconds. It was a thick, meaningful silence that felt more like a repression of words rather than just a lack of them. Clint looked around to see where this feeling was coming from and was about to shake the suspicion out of his mind completely until his eyes fell upon Mrs. Halliwell.

The elderly woman averted her eyes as soon as Clint tried to look at her. After years of playing poker, Clint knew better than to let such an obvious facial clue go by. Just to be sure, he kept looking at Mother Halliwell until she started to squirm slightly in place.

Clint nodded and looked away. He might have let her off the hook for the moment, but he wasn't about to forget it. The plan was to let her recover from what had happened before confronting her about what else she knew. With their lives hanging in the balance, as well as his own, he wasn't going to wait very long.

TWENTY-NINE

Roth sat in the darkness, surrounded on all sides by trees and shadows. His horse nosed what little grass it could reach while its tail swished back and forth behind it. Like the man on its back, the animal made almost no noise whatsoever, becoming instead just another part of the night.

Neither of them reacted to the gunshots they'd heard or even the voices raised in pain. As the smell of blood and gunpowder drifted toward them, Roth and his horse simply took more shallow breaths rather than take the acrid odors into their lungs. When quiet finally returned, he pulled back on the reins and prepared for what was to happen next.

By the time he'd collapsed the telescope he'd been using to watch the battle in front of the Halliwells' cottage, Roth heard the first rustlings of hurried footsteps closing in on his position. They came in from all sides, which told him that the men making the noise had lost all semblance of organization.

Roth made sure that there weren't going to be any unexpected visitors before riding his horse even farther back into the shadows. When he came to the spot where all the rest of the horses had been tied off, he climbed down from his saddle and waited for the first of his men to make themselves known.

Bursting from the trees, his face pale enough to show even in the near-total darkness, was one of the men that Frye had just taken on less than a month ago. When he saw that one's face, Roth was so angry that he couldn't even remember the man's name.

The gunman had been running straight for the horses, but when he saw that Roth was there as well, he altered his course so he could head straight for him.

"Where were you?" the gunman asked in a voice that cracked with panic. "We were all set up and in position, but you never showed. What the hell happened to you?"

When Roth knew that the gunman was finished talking, he took a step forward, grabbed hold of the front of his shirt and nearly yanked him off his feet. The other man struggled to maintain his balance, but was too shaken up to do much more than squirm in Roth's iron grip.

"You want to know where I was?" Roth sneered. "I was watching you men do everything but roll over and let yourselves get fucked like a couple of helpless bitches. *That's* where I was."

Roth's savage tone and harsh words caught the gunman off-guard. His eyes fluttered and his head twitched as though he was getting physically beat down by the barrage. When he opened his mouth to respond, all he could get out was a pathetic sputter.

"Shut your goddamn mouth," Roth ordered as he backhanded the other man across the face. "I sent in . . . what . . . six or seven men?"

"S-seven." As soon as he got the word out, the other man flinched as if expecting another smack.

"That's right. Seven men and still you couldn't take out a farmer and his family."

"Adams was with them. Clint Adams!"

"I don't care if it was Jesus Christ, you should have been able to get out of there with at least the kid and the mother." Pulling him in closer, Roth hissed, "I saw a couple men get into the house and signal that they had the family tied up. Didn't I see that?"

The gunman nodded, just as two more men broke into the clearing. When they first saw what was going on, they started to raise their guns. But once they knew who their partner was talking to, they holstered their weapons and came forward like a pair of scolded children.

Roth didn't take his eyes off the man directly in front of him for a second. His eyes still burned into that man as he used one hand to draw the .45 from where it had been hanging at his side. "You two," he said while jamming the gun beneath the first man's chin. "Explain why I shouldn't rid the world of you useless assholes right now . . . starting with this one right here."

The guy in Roth's grasp was still new to the group. Therefore, none of the others seemed all too anxious to jump to his defense, especially since they knew that Roth wasn't too good at bluffing.

"Well?" Roth asked.

Finally, one of the other two stepped forward. This one's shirt was soaked through with blood and he had to lean on the third man for support. The arm on his wounded side was tied up in a sling made from tattered material taken from the other man's coat.

"It was Adams . . ."

Roth snapped back the hammer and shook his head. "I don't want to hear that name. You were there before he was."

"We were and we waited there just like you told us. We had the mother and kid tied up and even had James and . . ." He paused for a second to reconsider his choice of words. "We had them outnumbered once they got there, but . . ."

"But what?"

The wounded man shook his head and shrugged, wincing in pain as even that simple gesture seemed to kick back on him. "Hell, Adams was too fast for us. There ain't a lot more for me to say."

Letting out a slow breath, Roth turned to face the wounded man and nodded. For the moment, the storm that had been brewing inside of him seemed to lapse. But just as soon as calm drifted across his face, his finger tightened around the trigger, blasting the top of the first gunman's head off in a spray of red mist. Roth let the twitching body drop like a piece of discarded refuse.

"I told you not to say that name," Roth said. "And when you don't follow orders *exactly* as I give them . . . this is what happens."

There was no gunshot echoing through the air, since most of the sound had been muffled by flesh and bone. Instead, there was only a heavy silence, which pressed down on the last two gunmen's shoulders like a lead weight.

"Take him to a doctor," Roth said to the one supporting his wounded partner. "Or drop him off the side of a mountain. I don't give a shit which."

"What should we say to Frye?"

"Nothing. I'll take care of that."

Glad to be dismissed for the moment, both gunmen moved toward their horses and started to climb into their saddles. While the wounded man was being helped onto his mount, another shot cracked through the air.

The wounded man felt a wet spray across the side of his face and when he turned to look around, he saw the man who'd been helping him fall dead to the ground. He didn't get a chance to even look in Roth's direction before one more shot sounded.

It was the last thing the wounded man ever heard.

The gun in Roth's hand was warm to the touch. A wisp

of dark smoke curled out from the barrel to put a bitter
taste in the back of his throat. He watched as the wounded
man hung from the side of his horse for a second or two
before his fingers finally lost their strength. The body hit
the ground on top of the other to form a neat pile at the
horses' feet.

Roth let out a sigh, went back to his own horse and
climbed into the saddle. He didn't wait to see if anyone
had heard those last two shots. It didn't even matter anymore. Instead, he put spurs to his horse's sides and
snapped the reins, taking off in a flurry of hooves to put
the grisly scene behind him.

THIRTY

"Is it done?"

Roth responded to the question with a shrug and a shake of his head. "I guess so."

Standing at the window in his office, Frye glanced over his shoulder. "You don't sound too happy. What went wrong?"

"I'm the only one who made it out."

Frye turned on the balls of his feet with his hands clasped behind his back. "Adams?"

"He killed most of them. Jim Halliwell took down Cobb."

"How could something like this happen?"

"They got cocky. And after that happened, they got sloppy. Them two don't usually make for a good combination."

The sound that came up from Frye's throat was one part sigh and another part growl. It curled his lip up just enough to show the glint of teeth, making him look like an animal that was about to snap at the closest hand he could reach. "And can you answer one question for me?"

Roth knew better than to say anything until the other man had spoken his piece.

"Tell me how all of my men are gone . . . and you somehow managed to come out of there alive." Frye's voice was strained and vaguely trembling. Veins were starting to pop out on his forehead and his color was turning even more pale than usual.

"Clint Adams," Roth replied. "He's fast. You knew that when you sent those men after him."

"But we had numbers on our side!"

"They were used to shooting at farmers and scaring shopkeepers, not dealing with men like Adams." Roth lowered his voice and added, "I'll find some more men. I know some that are nearby who are used to dealing with problems like these. In fact, I think one or two of them might have dealt with Adams before."

His face brightening somewhat, Frye eased himself into his chair and steepled his fingers. "Then find them. We need to take out the Halliwells before they leave town. If we don't, then I might as well hand over that ranch and kiss Lowry's money good-bye."

"You won't have to do that," Roth assured him. "Because part of that money is mine. Remember?"

"If you can help me pull this mess out of the fire, you'll have earned your share."

Roth nodded and turned toward the door. "You just sit back and let me round up my own crew. After that, you'll wonder why you never let me hire these men on when we first started. I'll take care of everything. Trust me."

Frye said nothing more. He let the gunman leave his office before getting back up and facing his favorite window. Watching Roth cross the street and head off, he wondered how this thing he'd started had gotten so damn far. By this point, it was even hard to remember how it had all began.

THIRTY-ONE

"Is it done?"

When Roth heard the question this time, he reacted in a much different way. His back was straight and his eyes were trained solidly on the man who'd asked it. Without the slightest bit of regret, he nodded once and said, "Yes, sir, Mister Evans. It went off without a hitch."

The fat man in the expensive suit clipped the end off a dollar cigar with a pair of small, silver-plated scissors. All he had to do was put the cigar to his mouth and Bullock was there with lit match in hand. Evans touched the tip of the cigar to the flame, took a few puffs and leaned back in his padded chair. "What about Frye's men?"

"They're all dead."

Evans raised his eyebrows. "Is that a fact? I have a man that says Adams didn't get to all of them before they took off running."

"Some of them got away from him, but they didn't get away from me."

The cigar glowed brightly as Evans inhaled. "Excellent," he said while releasing a gout of fragrant smoke. "So how many men does that leave our Mister Frye with?"

"Counting me," Roth said with a smirk, "one."

At first, Evans sounded as though a bit of tobacco had gotten caught in his throat. But the gruff scratching soon took on a different rhythm and then developed into a full-bodied laugh. "That's perfect. Absolutely perfect. Would you care for a cigar?"

Roth took a seat next to the fat man and stretched out. "Don't mind if I do."

Evans snapped his fingers and Bullock brought over another cigar. Instead of giving him the full treatment, however, the huge man tossed a tin match safe onto Roth's lap.

"What did you tell him?" Evans asked.

"I said I'd round up some men of my own to finish the job. He seemed to be pleased enough by that, but I don't think he'll sit back without lifting a finger of his own."

"Let him lift all the fingers he wants. It won't do a bit of good once you and my men start handling things. In fact . . . doubt very much that you'll even have to speak to Mister Frye again."

"So he's out of the picture altogether?" Roth asked.

"That's Mister Lowry's wish. He's getting way too big for those fancy britches he likes so much."

Roth took a moment to light up his cigar and get the ember burning. After letting the smoke roll around in his mouth for a bit, he exhaled and said, "So that just leaves Halliwell."

"Yes, it does. And the deed to the ranch is still in that family's possession, am I correct?"

Roth nodded.

"For some fool reason, Mister Halliwell hasn't accepted any of our offers to buy him out. I know why his father would never do such a thing, but since he passed, I figured the rest of the family would be more than happy to see the kind of money we were offering." The fat man's eyes narrowed and he chewed on the end of his cigar. "Maybe the rest of the family isn't as ignorant as I thought. That would explain a lot."

"Ignorant about what?" Roth asked.

Evans snapped out of his own thoughts and focused them back upon Roth. "Never you mind. Just take Bullock and some of my other men and get ready for your marching orders. We may have to clean out that cottage once and for all, but from here on out . . . you'd best cover your tracks. Mister Lowry doesn't want this to look like anything more than a local feud. His hands are dirty enough as it is."

Suddenly, the superior position Roth had felt he'd gotten after the night had gone so well wasn't looking so secure. When Evans glared at him, Roth felt like he was in more danger than when Frye had him at gunpoint. He didn't let any of this show, however. Like any other animal, he knew that Evans could smell fear.

"You did a good job tonight," Evans said, his voice taking on its cordial tone once again. Reaching into his jacket pocket, he took out a folded wad of money that was almost as thick as his own chubby finger. "Keep it up and there's plenty more where that came from."

Roth took the money and stashed it away.

"But if Mister Lowry doesn't get his hands on that deed," Evans said, "or if his name becomes connected to any of this dirty feud business, you might as well take that money and buy yourself a nice, comfortable coffin because that's where you'll be the moment you become more trouble than you're worth."

There wasn't a bit of cockiness in Roth's face as he got up and put his cigar out in a thick metal ashtray. And there wasn't the slightest trace of arrogance when he said, "I'll take care of this the right way, Mister Evans. You tell Mister Lowry that he won't have anything to worry about."

Evans didn't say a word. He simply waved his hand

toward Bullock and the giant man showed Roth to the door. It wasn't until the latch had shut and the gunman's steps could no longer be heard in the hallway outside that the fat man stirred from his spot.

Even the smoke hanging around his head had seemed to be waiting for a signal that it was safe to move again.

"What do you think, Bullock?" Evans asked. "Did old man Halliwell talk before he died?"

The big man's voice was a deep rumble. "I couldn't say since I never met the man."

"He was a pain in the ass, but at least he cooperated. He listened to reason and never gave us any trouble. Well . . . at least none that we couldn't handle."

"How many men should I take when I meet Roth?"

"All but one. I shouldn't need much security for the time being. I'm betting that the Halliwells are just about set to pull up their stakes here and move west. Once that happens, they can meet their end soon after. But don't wait too long. It's still got to look as though Frye was responsible for their deaths."

"Even Clint Adams?"

"Sure." Evans snorted. "Let him have his glory. That is . . . unless you'd rather have it?"

Bullock's eyes widened and his jagged mouth twisted into a vague parody of a smile. "I'd like that, Mister Evans."

"Fine. Consider it a bonus. Just make sure the body's found somewhere else. Like Oklahoma," he added while sending a smoke ring into the air. "We don't have any interests there."

THIRTY-TWO

Despite the shots that had echoed in the air not too long ago and the blood that still stained the ground, the Halliwells' cottage was relatively quiet. Clint had dragged away the bodies so they couldn't be seen right outside the window, hoping that James's little brother wouldn't be any more traumatized than he already was.

The rest of the family seemed to be handling everything rather well. Elena busied herself by tending to James, who spent the better part of the night asleep in bed. Although Mother Halliwell didn't want to blunt her son's pain with whiskey, she was a firm believer in the tonic she'd bought from a traveling salesman a few weeks ago.

Clint had to laugh at that, since that tonic probably knocked James onto his ass faster than twice that amount in whiskey. But he didn't have a problem with that, since James needed the rest. And he knew better than to say anything smart to Mother Halliwell, since she might just be able to knock a man out even faster than the tonic she'd bought.

Clint was resting his feet on the steps leading to the front of the house when the door swung open. Looking up, he saw Mother Halliwell shuffling outside, not even

129

worrying about the fact that Clint was sitting directly in her path.

Scooting to one side in the nick of time, Clint smiled as the old woman lowered herself onto the step next to him. She had the quiet authority that seemed to come with the territory of being a mother of more than one child. When she moved, she let others know what she wanted them to do without having to say a word. This resulted in a slightly gruff manner, but there was most definitely a kinder layer underneath the surface.

"I thought you might have gone to sleep already, Mrs. Halliwell," Clint said.

She coughed a few times into her hand and said, "I don't feel like I've been Mrs. Halliwell since my husband died. You might as well call me just plain Margaret."

"I'm sorry about what happened here. You've got yourself a real nice family, Margaret."

She'd been looking up at the stars when she'd first mentioned her husband. Still gazing up at the heavens, she swallowed hard and nodded slowly. "I know, Mister Adams. I know."

"If I get to call you Margaret, You should return the favor. It's Clint."

If she heard what Clint said, she didn't give him much of a sign. Instead, she just kept her eyes fixed on the sparkling lights above her as a tear rolled down one wrinkled cheek. She wiped it away with a hand that was just as wrinkled, yet somehow looked anything but frail. In fact, *frail* was not a word that could describe any facet of Margaret Halliwell.

Her body was short yet stocky and her movements were choppy yet precise. She never once cringed at the sight of blood, no matter how much of it had been spilled right in front of her eyes in the last couple of hours. Even what had happened to herself and her youngest son didn't break her resolve. She was still able to keep her head high and her eyes wide open.

"My family owes you a lot, Mister Adams. More than I'll ever be able to repay."

Clint was about to politely insist that she call him by his first name, but that innate authority in her tone kept his tongue in check. So he let her call him whatever she wanted, since fighting it would be a hopeless cause anyhow.

"I don't mind stepping in when I'm needed," he replied. "I'd hate to see anything happen to upstanding folks."

"You knew my daughter before all of this, didn't you?"

"Yes, ma'am."

"She spoke of you from time to time."

"Nothing that'll get me in any trouble, I hope."

With that, Clint was finally able to put a smile on the old woman's face and draw her eyes away from the stars. It wasn't much of a smile, but it was better than the sad frown that had been there before.

"I've got enough trouble for the both of us, I'd reckon," she said. "No need for me to start any more."

"That reminds me of something I'd like to ask you." Clint had been waiting for a better time to broach the subject, but he doubted if the perfect opportunity was going to present itself any time soon. That being the case, he went on as best he could. "I've got a feeling that you know more about what's going on here than you're letting on. Since you didn't seem to want to talk in front of James, I figured you might want to talk now."

"It's not James that I'm worried about so much as Evie. She was closer to her father than any of the rest. I doubt little Eddie barely even remembers his pa."

"About your husband's death—was he . . ."

"Killed?" Margaret said while Clint searched for a more delicate term. "No. He died as quiet as you please. One minute he was sitting in his chair out back watching the clouds pass by and the next he was just . . . gone. Nobody could ask to be taken up to the Lord's embrace in a more peaceful way."

"Like I said earlier, Margaret. There's something more going on here than just some men giving your son a hard time. Does it have anything to do with that ranch he inherited?"

The old woman turned her eyes so that she was looking directly at Clint. From that angle, it was almost as though he could see that something else was working inside of her beyond what she was letting on. Confirming that suspicion with a wink, she nodded once and looked back up to the night sky.

"You're a smart man, Mister Adams. From all I heard about you, I figured you as some gunfighter without a damn thing between his ears. Believe me, after spending most of my life with my husband, I know the type well enough.

"That ranch is sitting on a whole mess of trouble, that's for sure. But it's got nothing to do with the land it's on or that herd that runs out of there." The gruff edge came back to her voice when she added, "And it's got nothing to do with no damn view."

Clint nodded and looked up at the sky himself. "I knew it."

THIRTY-THREE

"Do you know anything about Peyton Lowry?" Margaret asked.

Clint started to give an automatic response, but then he stopped and thought about it for a second. "You know something? Besides the fact that he lives in Texas and has more money than he can count ... I really don't know that much about him."

As soon as she got onto the subject, the old woman looked down from the heavens and focused on the weathered boards beneath her stocky body. It almost seemed as though she couldn't hold her head up anymore now that she was thinking about this man.

"Well I never knew too much about him, myself." she went on to say. "I never really had much of a need to bother myself with details like keeping track of every rich man sitting on a fortune of money. But after living with my husband for a few years, I started to get real acquainted with Mister Lowry."

"Why's that?"

"At first, I thought he was just some old acquaintance of my husband's. I'd hear his name mentioned now and then, but it wasn't anything that really got my attention.

Like I said before . . . I never really knew too much about the man.

"But then Earl—that's my husband—started talking more and more about him. It really caught my attention when he started talking about some place out west where he might want to go to raise a family. Some ranch in Nebraska."

Clint heard the wind rustling through the nearby trees and his nerves reacted by sending a jolt of energy through his body. But as far as he could tell, the sound was just the wind doing what it normally does, and the energy came from a day spent dodging fists and bullets.

Margaret seemed to react in much the same way. She seemed worried at first, but then she simply pulled her shawl tighter around her shoulders and went on with her story. "I told him I didn't want to leave this town and all the folks I'd grown up with, so he dropped it for a while. But that subject always had a nasty habit of coming up every couple months or so. And every time it did, it got harder and harder for me to talk Earl out of picking up and heading west."

"What about the man that James told me about?" Clint asked. "I think his name was Kyle Bagley."

Margaret nodded. "We didn't meet Kyle till later. So far, what I'm talkin' about happened just before James was born. After that, Earl was too busy being a father to think about doing much of anything else for a while. Then when I was blessed with Elena, Earl seemed to forget about that ranch altogether."

"And he never told you anything about this place?"

"He was my husband, Mister Adams. And if you knew Earl, you'd know that he was always on the lookout to better himself and his kin. I never thought to question him too much about it. Not until Kyle showed up, anyways."

The wind was dying down, but Margaret still seemed cold. In fact, after mentioning Kyle's name, she started to

shiver just enough for Clint to notice that her shoulders
were trembling.

"The day I met Kyle Bagley was the day everything
changed," she said. "That was the day that things seemed
a little more complicated. Even my husband was a
changed man. He still loved his family, don't get me
wrong. But he wasn't as happy as when I fell in love with
him. He started looking over his shoulder and getting less
sleep at night.

"Whenever I asked him about it, he said there wasn't
nothing wrong, but I could tell there was. Finally, I
couldn't ignore it anymore and he couldn't come up with
any more explanations. He came clean and told me why
Mister Bagley kept coming by our place at odd hours of
the night and why he always brought so many armed men
with him."

Pausing for a second, Margaret started to look up at the
stars, but didn't seem quite ready to turn her eyes all the
way to the heavens. So she looked to Clint instead. "Bagley and Mister Lowry may have been partners, but they
were also the worst of enemies, you see. Earl told me that
he and Mister Bagley had worked out a deal of some kind
that would be in both of their interests."

Clint tried to sort something out in his head, but
couldn't quite do it on his own. "Wait a second," he said.
"Wasn't your husband friends with Peyton Lowry?"

"That's what I always thought. But it turned out that
Earl just bought this land from Mister Lowry," she said
while nodding toward the trees and ground surrounding
them. "This house, too," she added, patting the boards
beneath her. "When he finally took me into his confidence, Earl told me that he'd happened upon some papers
when he'd first moved into this place."

"What kind of papers?"

"The kind of papers that can make a man real rich real
fast, Mister Adams. The kind of papers that some men

keep because some other men would pay to have them
stay away from the law, or newspapers and such."

Finally, Clint was starting to see how some of these
pieces were fitting together. "You mean papers about
Lowry?"

"Not quite. They were papers about important men in
high places. Earl never told me exactly who, but he said
that it went all the way to Washington, D.C. He said that
if I knew any more, I'd just be in danger."

Clint sat speechless on the Halliwells' front steps. Although he figured there had to be something more going
on than just a simple feud, he hadn't thought for one moment that there could be *this much* going on. And when
he'd heard mention of Washington, D.C., he needed to
take a moment to digest it all.

Looking over at him, Margaret smirked slightly and
nodded. "Kind of takes your breath away, doesn't it?"

"Yeah. You could say that."

"Well, now you know what I've been living with for
all these years."

So many questions were popping into Clint's mind con-
cerning this situation. But the biggest one among them
was something that he kept thinking to himself again and
again: *What the hell have I gotten myself into*?

THIRTY-FOUR

"What does James know about all of this?" Clint asked when he finally had some of his thoughts straightened out inside his head.

Margaret shrugged. "Only what his father told him. Far as he knows, that ranch is nothing more than a ranch. It's prime property that can turn a good profit if worked the right way."

"He said that Lowry is looking to hire on someone to run the place."

"Actually, I'd say Mister Lowry is looking to replace my husband, who was more of a caretaker. You see . . . Mister Lowry stores a whole lot of dirty laundry at that ranch. Earl told me there's everything from bodies buried on the property to papers hidden beneath the floorboards."

"Just like this house?" Clint asked.

"Oh, much more than what was here. Mister Lowry came by to collect what he'd stored away here. That's when he took on my Earl as a caretaker. Since he already knew about this place, Mister Lowry asked him to keep the secret. Earl was an honest man and wouldn't have any of it, but Mister Lowry offered a whole lot of money. My husband was honest, but he had a growing family, you see.

"Still, Earl didn't like the idea of what he was to do, so Mister Lowry came by to collect everything that had been here . . . just some papers and such. Mister Bagley came here, too, figuring that Lowry wouldn't look too deep inside his own hiding place. He hid away just one thing of his own."

"Let me guess," Clint said. "The deed to the Nebraska ranch?"

"That's right. My Earl didn't know what was at that ranch and he didn't want to know. At least . . . not until Mister Bagley acquired it from Mister Lowry. He told Earl all about the things that had been here. He also said that the things at that ranch were twice as important."

"And that's right about the time your husband started to have troubles with his conscience."

Margaret nodded. She didn't have any trouble at all looking to the stars when she said, "Earl was a good man. He sat on what he knew for so long because Mister Lowry gave us a home and enough money to see us through the hard times most families have to go through every now and then. But Earl was still an honest man, God bless his soul, and he couldn't live with what he'd found out from Mister Bagley."

Watching the woman, Clint couldn't help but look up at the stars to see what was holding her attention. It was a clear night and the sky resembled an enormous sheet of black velvet dusted by flecks of diamond chips. He wasn't much of a religious man, but even Clint had to admit that an angel or two wouldn't look out of place up there.

"How did he know Mister Bagley could be trusted?" Clint asked after a few silent moments had gone by.

"Earl looked at those papers that were here, Mister Adams. After that, I guess he didn't have much of a reason to doubt that whatever was hidden in Nebraska could be just as bad . . . if not worse."

"And why did Bagley come forward with any of this?"

Another smile came onto her face. Only this time, there was no humor to be seen in the expression. If anything, it made the woman look a little darker around the edges. "He's a businessman, too. All he wanted was to be able to take down his rival when the time was right. Isn't that the way businessmen think, Mister Adams?"

Clint had no desire to become overly familiar with the workings of high finance and business affairs. But even though he was no expert on the subject, he knew enough to hear the ring of truth in what the widow was saying.

"Once my Earl came clean to me and I saw how much it was tearing him up inside, I decided to see if there was anything I could do to get him away from those people." Turning so that her shoulders were squared with Clint's and her entire body was facing his direction, she looked him dead in the eyes and explained, "I didn't care what those papers said and I still don't. All I know about them is that they were important enough to set these men against my husband just because Earl stumbled upon a loose floorboard when he was moving a table.

"It took every bit of strength I had, Mister Adams. But I was finally able to convince my husband to hide that deed away and stop taking their filthy money. The only reason Earl fought so hard was because he didn't want to deny me or our children anything that that money could buy."

She choked back some tears, but they seemed to be coming just as much out of anger than out of any sadness. "My Earl worked himself to an early grave to make up for what those rich bastards did to him."

"What did they do?" Clint asked.

"First, Lowry took the money away when he found out that Bagley had given him that deed. Then he got the banks to come after our land. Then he started paying someone in town to give us a hard time because he thought that Earl was set to take whatever was in that ranch for himself out of revenge or some such nonsense.

"Earl didn't have a vengeful bone in his body. And he wouldn't have even known about that ranch unless he'd been dragged into this mess by Lowry, himself. And when it was finally too much, Earl couldn't take no more. His heart gave out on him and took him away from me and the family that loved him so very much."

"What did he say to James?" Clint asked.

"He told James where the deed was and that there was a fortune to be made at that ranch."

"What about the herd?"

"That's what James thought his father meant by a fortune. None of the children knew about any of this. James is just trying to provide for us."

"And what about Frye? What's he got to do with any of this?"

"Far as I know, Frye's the one still working for Lowry."

"Does he know about any of this business with the papers or whatever's at the ranch?"

Margaret shook her head. "I don't think so."

"So Frye's just taking orders?"

The older woman shrugged.

Clint suddenly felt as though he'd eaten more than he could digest. Everything he'd learned was swirling around in his head like a continuous chattering voice. Bits and pieces fell into place here and there, but he still needed some time to sort it all out before he would even come close to ingesting it all.

"Mrs. Halliwell, I think James needs to know everything that's going on. After all he's been through, I think he deserves that much."

Margaret looked as though she was going to protest,

but then she stopped and nodded. "I guess you're right. All this time, I had just hoped I could talk him into leaving everything alone and let it pass by. That's how me and Earl had some of our most peaceful years together. I guess James is just more bullheaded than his father."

"Well, that bullheadedness might just start paying off."

Her eyes brightened a little bit when she said, "Really?"

"I hope so. But first . . . I've got to know who else knows about all of this."

"Lowry and whoever he trusts, of course. Then there's Bagley."

"Where can I find him?"

"Lord only knows. I haven't talked to him for some time. Some think he may be dead. But other than that . . . only me and Earl knew any of this. And Earl made sure that nobody knew about me."

"Good. The next thing we do is get James and Elena in here to clear the air. After that . . . we work out a way to clean this mess up once and for all."

"How can we do that?" Margaret asked hopefully.

Clint gave her a wry grin. "I haven't come up with that part yet."

THIRTY-FIVE

The sun was just cresting over the horizon by the time Margaret finished talking to her two oldest children. In the last few hours, she'd filled them in on everything she'd told Clint, as well as a few more things about their father that they'd never known.

Along the way, James and Elena went back and forth from being angry to speechless as they heard all the things that their mother had been keeping from them. On the other hand, Margaret seemed to be growing more energetic as the night wore on into day. Her eyes took on more of a sparkle as she unloaded all the things that had been weighing her down for so very long.

When she was done, Margaret fixed an early breakfast since everyone but the smallest child had been too worked up to even think about sleeping. As she prepared yet another pot of coffee along with eggs and bacon, the older woman finished up her confessions, leaving James and Elena more than a little dazed.

Finally, after downing a couple more sips of hot coffee, James was able to speak. "Jesus," he muttered.

Elena shook her head. Although she seemed to take what her mother had to say a little more in stride, she was

142

still baffled. "Yeah. I'd say that about covers it." Looking between Clint and her mother, she asked, "And how long has all of this been going on?"

"Ever since you were little," Margaret replied.

James took a deep breath. "And you were never going to tell me?"

"I thought it would just get you deeper into trouble. I thought I could get you to give Mister Frye what he wanted and then he'd leave us alone."

"Right. Now, he wants to kill me and take the rest of you hostage."

"True," Margaret said. "But you're also in this until the end and there's no backing out anymore. At least before I had hope for a better ending than that."

Clint helped himself to some of the eggs as well as a hearty portion of bacon. The smell of food was something that didn't make his head swim and it was nice to worry about something simple like breakfast for a change. "Well don't lose hope just yet," he said while sitting down to his place at the table. "There might be some way out of this."

"Thanks, Clint, but you've done more than enough for us," James replied. "This is a family matter and I can't ask you to get involved any more. Especially now that we know just how deep this thing runs."

"I've been thinking about that." As the sun started to shine through the window and the bacon started to crumble in his mouth, Clint felt as though he was getting his second wind. "We don't need to think about what those papers are or everything that's hidden in that ranch. If it was enough to build up Lowry's fortune, then it's got to be something pretty big.

"As far as something involving Washington, D.C., I've met enough politicians to know that they don't get too high up on the ladder without collecting some dirt under their fingernails. There might be dirt on senators or even

the president at that ranch. My point is, what's there
doesn't matter and trying to figure it out is a waste of
time and energy. All that does matter is that Lowry wants
to protect that dirt and somebody else wants to get it. Am
I right?"

Hearing things boiled down to such basic terms did
everyone gathered around the table a lot of good. Suddenly, things didn't seem so overwhelming. One by one,
the Halliwells shrugged and nodded.

"That sounds about right," Margaret said, speaking for
the rest of her family as well.

"Then the problem is pretty simple," Clint continued
between bites. "All we need to do is deal with both sides
until each one is taken care of. Now, there's Lowry's men
and Frye's men, so let's start with the smaller group."

"That'd be Frye's," Margaret stated.

"So that means he also has the most to lose. He'll also
be more desperate right about now because of what's happened since I've arrived. And desperate men are the best
kind to work with in these kind of situations. No matter
what, you can always figure that a desperate man will
either fight or run."

Clint took another bite and swallowed before going on.
"That leaves us with Lowry. We know what he wants as
well as what he'll do to get it. So the way I see it, since
Frye is running low on manpower, there's one simple way
out of this entire mess."

Before Clint could finish his train of thought, Margaret
slapped the table and smiled brightly. "Get to that ranch,"
she said triumphantly.

James blinked and shifted his eyes back and forth between Clint and his mother. "I don't get it."

"It's too late to back away and take whatever Lowry's
offering," Clint said. "I have a hunch that he might be
stirring up this feud between you and Frye just because
he figures you'll lose and he wants you out of the picture."

"Then why didn't he just come after me himself?"

This time, it was Elena who spoke up. "Because that would draw attention to himself. If Daddy found things that he used for blackmail, then Lowry doesn't want the law looking at him too hard." Glancing to Clint, she asked, "Right?"

Clint nodded. "That's right. If he's tried to kill you once, then the only thing he can do is keep trying until he either succeeds or runs out of reasons to keep trying."

"And if we get to that ranch and get rid of whatever's there," Margaret said, "then he can leave us in peace."

James looked as though he finally had things worked out inside his own head. "I can be there in a few days if I ride as fast as I can."

Clint cut him off sharply. "No. Frye's watching you and so is Lowry's man here in town. I'll go. My horse can make the trip faster than anything you've got. It'll get a whole lot messier before it's over, but at least it'll be over."

Everyone seemed to be happy to finally figure out something they could do besides just sit back and wait for the next attack to come. Everyone, that is, except for Elena. She returned James's smile, but couldn't hide the sadness behind her eyes.

THIRTY-SIX

Clint was tending to Eclipse around the back of the Halliwells' place when Elena came up to him. The Darley Arabian stallion was in prime condition for a run, which was exactly what Clint had been hoping for. Before he could feel comfortable setting off on any type of ride, he had to make sure Eclipse was watered and fed.

"That's a fine animal," Elena said as she walked up close enough to run her hand along Eclipse's mane.

Pouring some feed in a wooden bin, Clint nodded and said, "He's gotten me through quite a bit." When he was done with the feed, he set the bag aside and turned to face Elena. "All right. Out with it."

"Out with what?"

"Something's been bothering you since breakfast, so why don't you just tell me what it is? It'll make you feel a whole lot better."

Elena seemed to know what she wanted to say, but just couldn't get the strength to spit it out. Finally, after pulling in a deep breath, she said, "Frye wants to kill you."

"So tell me something I don't know."

"That's why you're going. And that's why you don't want my brother to go with you, isn't it?"

"Look. This is one hell of a mess your family's gotten themselves into. If I would have known more going in, I might have been able to help a lot more. But it's past a certain point and blood's been spilled. When that happens, you've got to see it through to the end or else it'll be the end of you."

At that particular moment, Clint wasn't sure if he was saying those things for Elena's benefit or his own.

"I know what your plan is," she said. "You want to bring Lowry's attention to you so that he'll leave us alone. I know you can protect yourself, but this might be too much even for you to handle on your own."

"The next time James gets into a fight, he might not be so lucky. If I would've known how much there was at stake, I would have tried to protect him more." Clint was tightening the straps on his saddle and he suddenly felt like tearing the straps apart and throwing the rig onto the ground. "As it is, James can't use one of his arms and who knows how close you came to catching a bullet."

Elena could tell that Clint was getting madder with each passing second. Some of that anger eased up a bit when she put her arms around him and rested her head on his shoulder. "Don't blame yourself for what happened to James. It's not your fault you didn't know what was going on. None of us knew. Well . . . except for Mother."

Clint might have felt a little better, but he was still uneasy. "This mess isn't going to end unless we bring it to an end. And since James only has one arm to use for the time being and he wouldn't even stand much of a chance against those gunmen with both arms, that leaves me."

"But you didn't ask to be in any of this," Elena said. "I'm the one who dragged you here."

"Don't fret about it too much. If I'd have seen what was happening to James in town, I would have stepped in the same way I did before." Looking down into her eyes, Clint smiled and added, "I kind of have a way of getting drawn into these things no matter what I do."

"We'll find a way to deal with Frye . . . or Lowry . . . or whoever we need to deal with."

"I told you already, it's too late to deal. Too many people know about what's going on and Lowry's safest bet is to just cut off all the loose ends rather than worry about who will say what to whom."

"So that's it? You're riding to that ranch to get those papers?"

Clint stopped what he was doing and held Elena at arm's length. He kept quiet while thinking about something that seemed to occupy all of his attention. Finally, he leaned in close to her ear and whispered, "Can I trust you with something?"

Although Elena was still distraught, her interest was piqued by Clint's tone. "Of course you can."

"This is something that involves your entire family and their safety. All of their lives are in trouble now, so—"

"I know what's at stake, Clint," she interrupted. "Just tell me how I can help."

THIRTY-SEVEN

Roth had been sitting in the saddle for so long now that his entire lower body was starting to go numb. His upper body wasn't doing much better and pain was shooting all throughout his spine. Besides that, the chill carried by the morning air was chewing at the tips of his fingers and nose like some invisible carnivorous rodent.

But no matter how much it had pained him to sit in the trees surrounding the Halliwell cottage until the break of dawn, it was all worth it when he saw Clint Adams say his goodbyes and ride away. Just to be sure, he tagged along behind Adams for a mile or two, hanging back just far enough to keep the other man in sight without being spotted himself. There were plenty of ways to shadow the trail he was using without being in the open and Adams seemed to be in too much of a hurry to check his tail more than once or twice anyway.

Moving again, even though he was still in the saddle, was good for Roth's aching bones. And being sure that Adams was headed west in one hell of a rush did wonders for Roth's mind.

Finally that one was leaving town. Finally things would get back to normal.

No, the gunman corrected himself, not normal. Better than normal. With Adams away, this business could get wrapped up before the day was out. Frye would be finished. Lowry would be happy and Roth would have more money than he'd ever had in his life.

The very thought of it brought a smile to his face.

But before he could celebrate any further, he needed to head back to town and report the good news to Evans.

"Bullock and the rest of the men are ready to go," the fat man said as soon as Roth entered his suite at the Hilltop Lodge. "The only thing they were waiting for was your signal." Stepping up so that he was nose to nose with the gunman, Evans said, "it never came."

Roth took a reflexive step back. Although Evans wasn't as physically imposing as some of the killers in his employ, he had an intimidating way about him that hit Roth on an instinctual level.

"I can explain that," Roth said.

"I should damn well hope so."

"Adams and Mrs. Halliwell were talking last night. I got close enough to hear just about everything they said."

Evans looked suspiciously at the man before him. "How could you hear what they said? Am I supposed to believe you just pulled up a chair and—"

"No, no. I've lived in these parts most of my life. I know these woods like the back of my hand. They were talking in the middle of the night and I got close enough to make out most of it."

That seemed to satisfy Evans . . . at least for the moment.

"The old woman said a lot of things. She knows everything that's going on. She also knows some things I haven't even heard yet."

Anger flashed in Evans's eyes and his muscles tensed as though he was about to lash out at the first thing he could reach. "Which is all the more reason my men should have been there to take care of them," he snarled through clenched teeth.

Again, Roth took a step back. This time, he raised his hands to waist level as though he was getting ready to defend himself. "But that's the thing. Adams was there with them. You know what he can do. If we would have gone in there last night, we would have had to deal with him."

"And how is that different now?"

Before Roth could answer, a commotion sounded from another part of the hotel. A woman's voice could be heard screaming something and several male voices came back in response.

"What the hell is going on?" Evans asked.

Roth looked around. "Sounds like it was coming from outside." Taking advantage of the excuse to get away from the fat man, Roth opened the door to the hallway and poked his head out. The voices immediately became louder only this time, they were accompanied by heavy footsteps thumping against the floorboards.

"If you want to kill us, just do it now!" came the woman's voice.

The footsteps got louder and seconds later, Bullock was filling up the doorway with his huge, bulky frame. "The Halliwell woman is in the lobby," he said to Evans. "She's making a fuss about what happened the other night."

"Shut her up! How the hell did she know we were even here?"

"She wasn't asking for you, sir."

"What?"

"It's Frye. He's downstairs, too, and he's the one she's giving hell to."

"Really?" Evans said in a way that took away a healthy portion of the aggression that had been his face and turned it into a strange sort of curiosity. "Well, this is something I'd like to see."

THIRTY-EIGHT

When Evans stepped out into the hall, he was immediately assaulted by a woman's screams. Spouting off in an angry barrage of threats and accusations, she would occasionally break into a high-pitched shriek that had a way of seeping through the cracks of every wall in the hotel.

Evans stopped at the railing near the top of the stairs so he could look down onto the lobby. Surprisingly enough, all of his own men were positioned around the staircase and the lobby as if to give the woman her space. Taking center stage in front of the attractive Halliwell was a face that was very familiar indeed to Evans. And since Frye looked even more flustered than Evans had imagined, he was very pleased indeed.

"You murdering son of a bitch!" Elena shrieked while storming toward Frye. "How dare you show your face in this town after what you did! My brother never did a thing except try to give us a better life and you try to kill him for it!" That last word was punctuated by a wide swing of her right fist, which damn near caught Frye in the jaw.

Looking around to the men gathered nearby, Frye said, "Would somebody get this woman away from me? I'm here on my own business and she—" He stopped in mid-sentence when he caught sight of Roth standing at the top of the stairs. "You! Get your ass down here right now! What the hell are you doing here when I told you to take care of . . . that job for me?"

Roth shrugged and looked around at the other gunmen. "How'd you find me?"

"I saw you walking in here, that's how," Frye shot back. "I thought we had an arrangement."

"We did have an arrangement," Roth answered. "But it's over now. I found a better one."

It took a few seconds for Roth's words to fully sink in. Once they did, Frye glared around at the people standing in the lobby as the entire picture came into focus. When he spotted Evans at the balcony overlooking the scene, Frye nodded slowly. "I get it now. Lowry sent his dog to turn my own people against me."

Roth started walking slowly down the stairs. "Maybe you weren't listening to me the last time we spoke. You don't have any more people, Zeke. They're all dead. All except for me."

"That's right. And now you belong to Lowry. Or do you just take orders from that fat pig up there?"

As soon as Frye said that, a sound rushed through the lobby that resembled the flap of thick, leathery wings followed by the snapping of nearly half a dozen pistol hammers. Frye looked around to see that all the gunmen who had been standing nearby were all now glaring at him over polished barrels.

Even Elena had been shocked into silence once she was aware that so much firepower was on the verge of going off.

Feeling completely in his element, Evans walked down the stairs with slow, thumping steps. Pushing past Roth, he said, "You're done here, Frye. You were supposed to be running this town for Mister Lowry and you couldn't even keep a few locals in line. Once some hotshot blows into town, you go to pieces and get your entire crew killed off."

Unconcerned with what Frye was doing, Evans walked straight over to Elena. "And what brings you here today?"

Taking a deep breath, Elena fought through her nervousness. "I've got nothing left to lose." Once she started talking, the anger that she'd been feeling came back to put some more power behind her words. "It's plain to see that you're going to kill me and my family and I'm sick of running."

"But I thought Mister Adams was doing such a wonderful job of protecting you."

"He's gone. He went to that ranch in Nebraska to get his hands on whatever it is that your boss thinks is so damn important. Once he gets it, he'll ruin you."

"And he just left you here unprotected?" Evans asked. "I haven't known the man for very long, but that seems out of character."

"I told him we could stay hidden until he got back. I told him whatever I had to or else he wouldn't have gone. But he had to go. Even if he killed all of you, Lowry would just send more. This has to end."

"Very true. So you came here to gloat? Or did you just feel like screaming at us?"

"I came to beg for our lives."

If anything, Evans seemed genuinely amused by that. Nodding, he went over to where Frye was standing and said, "If you want to beg, then you're not going about it in a very productive way. You need to be more sincere. I know . . . let Frye here show you the proper way to beg."

Frye looked as though he was about to snap at any moment. His hand wavered over his gun and he shifted nervously from one foot to another. All the while, his eyes flicked around the room as if he was constantly counting all the guns pointed at him.

"Go on, Frye," Evans said. "Show Miss Halliwell the proper way to beg for your life."

For a second, Frye's expression was tainted by the same pride he'd shown when he used to walk through the streets of Barryville as if they were his own. He held his chin up and puffed his chest out while the hand hovering over his gun suddenly became steady. "I don't beg for no man," he said.

Turning to Elena, Evans said, "You see what pride does to a man? It fills his head full of big notions and makes him do stupid things. Pride is what brought this whole situation to this unfortunate conclusion."

Despite how much Elena truly hated Frye and all that had been done to her family, she couldn't bear the thought of seeing what was about to happen. "Y-you don't have to do this," she stammered.

Evans looked at her and then looked around to his men. "Actually," he said while snapping his fingers, "this is exactly what I have to do."

As soon as he got the words out, four guns went off within the lobby. The shots were timed with such precision that they sounded like only one pistol had been fired. Each bullet found its place in Frye's head and chest, killing him before he hit the floor.

THIRTY-NINE

Evans snapped his fingers again, causing Elena to flinch and cover her head with her hands. But instead of another round of gunfire, all that came was the sound of leathery wings once again as all the shooters put their weapons away.

"Now, Miss Halliwell," Evans said. "Why don't you tell me again where Mister Adams went off to."

This time, she didn't have any anger left to steady herself. All she felt was stark fear for her life, which caused her breath to catch in her throat and all the blood to run from her cheeks. "H-he headed w-west."

Evans sounded anything but trusting when he asked, "Are you sure about that?"

"She's right." It was Roth who spoke as he moved the rest of the way down the stairs to move in closer to Evans. He was stopped before he could get too close by Bullock's hamlike hand on his shoulder. "I was going to tell you myself. I followed Adams after he left the Halliwell place. He took the trail out of town and headed west. I heard him say something about riding hard all the way to Nebraska and by the looks of it, that's exactly what he was doing."

Although he seemed skeptical at first, Evans stared into Roth's face as though he could see all the way down to the gunman's soul. Glancing over to one of his own personal killers, he asked, "Anyone else seen Adams around?"

The killer shook his head. "No sir."

"In that case, maybe I'll head on out to that cottage I've been hearing so much about. That way I can see things for myself, make sure that all of Mister Lowry's belongings are accounted for so we can clear out of this place once and for all."

"What about my family?" Elena asked.

Evans winked and said, "Don't worry about them. I'll be sure to make it quick and painless." He snapped his fingers and before the woman could even put up much of a struggle, she felt hands closing in around both her arms.

"Nothing personal, you understand. But my employer has had his fill of dealing with your family. He might be getting soft in his old age, but I'm sure even he won't argue too much when I tell him that you're all dead and buried."

Elena started to scream, but one of those hands that had come from behind clamped over her mouth before she could get out more than a peep.

Leading the way, Evans walked to the front door of the hotel and stepped outside. Once there, he filled his lungs with fresh air and pat both hands against his belly. "You did good, Michael," he said as Roth stepped outside. "Mister Lowry appreciates good help and he's always got a space for a man like you."

"Thank you, Mister Evans."

"Think nothing of it. You can start your service by having a word with the good sheriff over there," he said, pointing to the lawman who Roth hadn't even seen yet. "Assure him our business here is almost done and that it would be in his best interests to let us conclude it and be on our way."

Roth locked eyes with the lawman. He knew Sheriff Williams wasn't the boldest of men, but he had been known to fight when painted into a corner. Killing Frye in broad daylight along with everything else that had happened in the last day or two was a pretty cramped corner, indeed.

"And what if he doesn't want to step aside?" Roth asked.

"After seeing what happened to the last person who gave me trouble, do you really have to ask that question?"

In his mind, Roth could already hear the snap from the fat man's fingers, which could end Sheriff Williams's life just as easily as it could end his own. Nodding once, Roth stepped down off the boardwalk and into the street. "Yes sir, Mister Evans."

When Roth started walking toward the sheriff, he noticed that a crowd was gathering around the hotel. Attracted by the sounds of Elena's screaming as well as the gunshots, the locals stood by with their eyes wide taking in the grim procession emerging from the hotel.

The lawman gathered up his courage and started walking toward Roth as well. "This has gone on far too long," Williams said. "All of you men are going to have to—"

"They're all going to finish their business here and leave," Roth interrupted. Suddenly, the gunman's attention was drawn to something he spotted from the corner of his eye. Just that small glimpse was enough to put him on edge so much that he instantly went for the .45 at his waist.

The sheriff reacted to that and went for his own Peacemaker.

But even though Roth cleared leather first, he didn't aim at the sheriff. Instead, he turned on his heel toward the familiar face that had caught his eye a second ago.

"Is this everyone?" Clint asked as he stepped out from the crowd. "Because I'm getting awful tired of trying to keep track of you all."

FORTY

Now, Roth's eyes were as wide as the rest of the locals who'd gathered in huddled clumps along the street. "But . . . but I saw you ride out of here," he said. "I saw you get on your horse and head toward Nebraska."

"You saw me do all that," Clint replied. "Just like I saw you following me the entire way. Just like I saw you skulking in the shadows damn near every time there was a shooting. Hell, even a blind man had a good chance of seeing you when you were trying to listen in on me and Mrs. Halliwell."

Roth looked between the sheriff and Evans, unsure as to what he should do next.

Glancing over to Evans, Clint said, "And by the looks of things, I'd guess that you're the man Lowry sent. I figured you'd show your face once you were fairly certain that your hired guns had cleared the way for you. It's pretty easy to play the big man when the only ones you haven't bought out yet are a woman, her wounded brother, an old lady and a child. But then again . . . I see you're used to being the biggest man in most places, aren't you?"

This time, the gunmen around Evans weren't so quick

160

to draw their weapons. Instead, they looked to their boss for direction.

Without batting an eye, Evans bared his teeth and pointed to Roth. "You know what to do," he said to the gunman. *"Now do it!"*

The sheriff was watching this with confusion swimming in his eyes. His gun was in hand, but he had yet to pull back the hammer. Making his decision in a heartbeat, Roth turned at the waist so he could squeeze off a shot at the lawman and turn back around before Clint had a chance to draw.

Before he could even get his barrel aimed in the sheriff's direction, however, he heard the sound of steel brushing against leather, followed by the crack of a single shot.

Still drawing a breath, Roth tried to take his shot, but found that his arm didn't want to follow the desperate orders coming from his brain. Pain shot through his shoulder, announcing the fresh bullet hole that had been punched through his flesh and bone.

Clint's Colt was smoking in his hand. Waiting for the momentum of his first shot to spin Roth around, Clint picked out a clean shot and took it. The next round drilled straight through Roth's heart, dropping the gunman just as the sheriff was about to pull his own trigger the first time.

Roth's face was covered with stunned surprise. He dropped to his knees and fell facefirst onto the street.

Turning to look at Evans, Clint held his Colt at waist level and said, "Have your men let Elena go and I might just let you walk out of here. You hurt one hair on her head, and you'll be taken back to Lowry in a pine box."

"You can do whatever you like, Mister Adams," Evans said with a confidence that was almost convincing. "Mister Lowry is a powerful man. He'll get what he wants whether you kill me or not. And when he finds out about the part you played in all of this, he'll kill you as well."

"That's pretty tough talk coming from someone sweating a river through his clothes."

"Torment me all you like. That doesn't change the facts."

Next to Clint, Sheriff Williams was getting his wind back after coming a hair's width away from taking a bullet. The lawman started to lift his gun and step forward, but he was stopped by a quick wave from the man who'd saved his life.

"Keep an eye out, Sheriff," Clint whispered. "But don't move until I do. Think you can back me up?"

Looking down at Roth's body, Sheriff Williams glanced back to Clint and nodded sharply.

Already, some of Evans's killers were starting to make a move. But they stopped short when Clint looked back in their direction, knowing that they would only get one chance to take him on before they wound up like Roth.

Evans still had to take a single step back toward the hotel. Watching him carefully, Clint wasn't sure if the fat man was dumber or braver than he'd originally thought. At the very least, Evans wasn't going to rush into a fight when he wasn't sure he could win.

"All right," Evans said. "You got me out into the open and you caught my men off their guard. What do you hope to accomplish here today, Adams?"

"I've heard enough about that ranch in Nebraska. And I've heard enough about whatever blackmail Lowry has hidden away."

"Do you even know what Mister Lowry has in that ranch?"

"Not exactly," Clint replied. "And I couldn't care less. Whatever dirty business he's got going won't be stopped by me. I know that much for sure. But I also know that the Halliwells are going to have to pay for that dirty business with their lives. They didn't ask to be pulled into this mess and it's too late for you to just let them out."

Evans nodded slowly. "It takes a wise man to know when he's facing a losing battle."

"Shut that mouth and open your ears," Clint said sharply. "The Halliwells are no longer a problem of yours . . . and neither is that ranch."

Laughing under his breath, Evans said, "All I need to do is send one telegraph and I'll have men cleaning out that ranch. I would've done it earlier, but I didn't want to scare any of these little rabbits away if they decided to run for it to their new home. Now that this little family is all in one place, I can rid myself of that ranch once and for all. I'm sure it won't be too difficult to find someone to watch over those materials just like old man Halliwell used to."

Clint let the fat man's words hang in the air for a few moments, giving Evans just enough time to let the superior smirk shine brightly amid his multiple chins. Once the gunmen scattered about started to look comfortable as well, Clint shattered their sense of well-being with one sentence.

"You're not the only one who can use a telegraph," he said.

FORTY-ONE

"What did you say?" Evans asked.

"While I was circling back into town during my morning ride, I placed a cable of my own," Clint replied with a wry grin. "I know people too. And I'm sure as soon as my friend gets that message, he won't have any problem with riding out to that ranch and poking around beneath the floorboards. In fact . . . I'd say he's on his way right now."

Evans glared at Clint through slit eyes as his nostrils flared with rage. "You're bluffing."

"I don't care if you believe me or not. I just thought I'd save you the heart attack when you found out for yourself. Besides, since you look like you're about to bust out of that suit, I'd say you believe me just fine."

For the first time since any of his men had been around him, Evans was truly at a loss for words. Bullock had to look twice at his boss just to make sure that the fat man wasn't about to keel over on the spot.

Clint took full advantage of the commotion he'd created by taking a step toward Evans and his men. Sheriff Williams, although shaken and wound up tighter than a watch, fell into step right beside him.

"That brings us back to the beginning," Clint said. "Let the woman go."

The killers holding onto Elena's arms and covering her mouth looked over to their boss to see if he would give the order. But Evans merely stood in his tracks, his massive body trembling with enough built-up anger to power a steam engine.

Clint knew that this was the moment where he had to be most on his guard. In a poker game, this would have been the moment where he'd shown his hand and beat a man out of his life savings. Some men took their losses in stride, while others tipped the table over, drew their guns and went for broke.

Even after what he'd seen of the fat man, Clint was hard-pressed to say which way Evans was going to go.

"Whatever was in that ranch is gone now," Clint said evenly. There was no threat in his voice. It was just a simple statement of fact. "I don't care what it is and I don't want to do anything with it. But it's gone and your boss doesn't have any more reason to come after this family. If he does, I might just take a gander at those papers and deliver them to whoever might be interested in reading them."

Evans was pale as a ghost. His blubbery lips moved slightly as he started to speak, but they never parted far enough to let any words out.

Every moment that passed made Clint more uncomfortable. If this was going to end well at all, it had to end quickly. With that in mind, he set his last card onto the table.

"And if you're thinking about how Lowry can get you out of this mess," Clint said, "I'd think back to how many times he told you to keep this matter quiet and out of the public eye."

Clint could almost hear that last sentence click into place within the fat man's head. Evans looked at him with an impressive poker face, but there was no way for him to hide the fact that he'd been affected by what Clint had just said.

"You don't know what Mister Lowry told me," Evans pointed out.

"Maybe not," Clint said, pressing his advantage, "but I think it's safe to say that he didn't go through all this trouble for so many years to have someone sitting on those papers if he didn't want to be discreet. I don't know Lowry as well as you do, but I know he's not widely known as an outlaw. Unless he might have changed over the years, of course. Does he make it common knowledge that his men kill people in broad daylight?"

Clint panned his eyes from side to side, noticing that Evans did the same. "Take a good look at these people," he said. "Because they're all taking a good look at you. What are you going to do, Evans? Kill them all? Was that Lowry's orders? Or do you think it would be easier for him to write you off and deny he's connected to any of this tangled web that's been spun around this place and this family?"

Evans started to shake his head. The movement was slow at first, but within seconds, he was looking around and shaking his head faster and faster as if he was working to deny what a fix he was in. He started backpedaling then, each step he took shakier than the one before it.

"No, no, no," Evans moaned. "You've said enough, Adams. Shut your mouth!"

"You know I'm right," Clint pressed on. "Just like you know that you're finished. Turn yourself over to the sheriff here, because that's the only way you're getting out of here alive."

"No! No, no, no!"

"Lowry will get to you sooner or later."

Evans couldn't deny the facts any longer. Looking around to his men, he snapped his fingers and shouted, "Kill him!"

FORTY-TWO

"Kill the woman!" Evans shouted in a voice dripping with desperate panic. "Kill anyone you have to! Just wipe them out!"

Clint felt like he'd been standing in the middle of a set of train tracks as the sound of a steam engine was approaching from half a mile away. Watching Evans this entire time and pushing him further and further toward his breaking point, he knew that the train was about to roll him over. Fortunately, he was more than ready to jump.

The first target that Clint picked out from among the hired killers was the man holding a gun to Elena's head. In one fluid motion, Clint drew his Colt and fired. The bullet whipped through the air and hissed over the heads of two other gunmen, causing them to drop to the ground. It found its mark in the forehead of the gunman standing directly behind Elena, clipping off a piece of his skull and snuffing out his life like wet fingers pinching a candle's wick.

The blood from that first hit was still spraying through the air when Clint shifted his aim slightly to one side and fired again. This time, the bullet took a course that only varied from the first shot by a few degrees. It kept those two killers close to the ground, since they had no way of knowing if he was firing at them or not.

Instead, Clint's second shot whipped through the air and punched through the left eye of the gunman who'd been holding onto Elena's other arm and covering her mouth. It snapped that man's head back almost hard enough to break his neck and he was dead before he even knew he'd been hit.

From Elena's vantage point, all she saw was a sudden flurry of activity as Clint took two shots in her direction. In the space of a second, the air around her was alive with the lethal passage of hot lead and the men on either side of her were picked off like clay pigeons.

For a second, Elena thought that she was dead. There was blood on her arms and some on her shoulders. But when she realized that none of that blood was her own, she fought back the urge to scream while stepping over the bodies, which were now piled around her feet. Elena held her head down low and ran back into the hotel as quickly as she could.

Once Clint saw that Elena had had enough sense to find some cover, he turned his attention back to Evans's gunmen. There were four more closing in around the fat man as if to shield him and there was one giant of a man charging toward Clint without casting so much as a concerned glance toward the smoking Colt in his hand.

Without having to rely on anything but pure instinct, Clint took aim and fired at the oncoming Bullock. He could see that his shot hit the big man in his mid-torso, but that was only because he could see the splash of blood popping from his flesh. Other than that, there was nothing.

Bullock didn't slow down.

He didn't turn away.

He didn't even flinch from the pain or the sound of the gunshot.

He just kept coming.

Another shot fired next to Clint. This once came from Sheriff Williams. It was quickly followed by another as well as return fire coming from the hired guns.

Lead hissed through the air all around him, but all Clint could see was the figure of Bullock, which kept growing larger and larger as he got closer and closer. Clint was about to take another shot, but the big man lashed out with a hand in a surprising burst of speed, knocking the Colt out of his grasp.

Knowing that it would be a mistake to concern himself with retrieving his weapon at that particular moment, Clint instead focused on the giant in front of him. Bullock's teeth were clenched and he let out a rumbling breath as he swung his other hand in a looping arc with the sole intention of separating Clint's head from his shoulders.

It was all Clint could do to duck in time as Bullock's hamlike fist swiped over him. The blow knocked the hat right off of Clint's head and clipped the top of his skull. Even though it was a glancing shot, there was still enough power in it to make Clint unsteady on his feet for a second or so. Crouching down with a close-up view of Bullock's chest and stomach, Clint balled up his fists and hammered away at the other man.

It felt as though he was trying to knock down a brick wall with his bare hands and Clint soon realized that his knuckles were probably hurting more than anywhere he'd hit Bullock. Clint managed to get in four or five quick shots before he could see the other man stretching up as though he was arching his back.

Bullock was actually straightening up and lifting both hands over his head. His fists looked like massive sledgehammers and were both swinging down toward Clint's face.

Reflexively, Clint lifted both arms up to shield himself, knowing full well that he wouldn't be able to throw himself out of the giant's reach. There was no way he could brace himself enough to absorb the impact as both fists came crashing down onto his arms, driving them both back into himself.

Bullock's forearms smashed against Clint's attempt to block. When he felt that he'd driven the smaller man down like a spike being pounded into the dirt, Bullock used his left hand to scoop Clint's arms down while coming in with a vicious right.

Even though his own strength was fueled by the adrenaline pumping through his body, Clint could do nothing to keep his arms from being swatted aside. It seemed as though he could stand back and watch as the next blow came toward him, since he was almost as helpless as someone casually observing the fight.

When the fist landed, it caught Clint on the side of his face. If he hadn't turned his head away at the last second, Clint's nose might have been pushed all the way into the back of his skull. As it was, his head snapped violently to one side and the world around him became nothing more than a gray mess.

Clint felt as if he was looking up from the bottom of a dirty river. The only thing he could see clearly was the little splatter of blood on Bullock's side. Even as everything else began to blur, that bloodstain remained in focus. He knew that was his brain showing him the only way he was going to make it away from this man in one piece.

Knowing better than to second-guess his instincts, Clint twisted his body to one side, clenched his hands together and swung them upward. With his fingers laced between each other, both of Clint's hands were about the same size as one of Bullock's.

But the size of his fists didn't matter. All that mattered was that Clint's last-ditch shot landed squarely on that splatter of blood, pounding against the bullet he'd put into the big man moments ago.

Clint's knuckles slammed against something wet and slick. When he followed through with the blow, he actually felt Bullock stumble back as a pained howl churned up from deep within the giant's chest.

For a second, Clint thought he might have been seeing things. But the big man was indeed stumbling back, clamping one of those humongous fists to the weak spot that had just exploded.

Clint dropped down to one knee, his hand groping for the spot where he remembered his Colt had dropped. If his eyes and ears were jangling erratically after taking so much punishment, at least Clint's memory was still in working order. His fingers wrapped around the Colt's handle and he brought up the gun just as Bullock was starting to stampede toward him a second time.

Knowing he probably couldn't survive another hand-to-hand battle with the giant, Clint pointed his barrel and squeezed off two shots in quick succession. The first drilled through Bullock's heart and the next two turned his face into a bloody pulp.

Clint's hands worked with practiced fluidity as he emptied the Colt and began slipping fresh rounds into the cylinder. Since Bullock was still wobbling on his feet, Clint used the big man as cover while he tried to blink away the fog that still clouded his head.

FORTY-THREE

Clint was just snapping the cylinder shut when his cover finally dropped over onto the street. What he saw when his view cleared was not exactly what he'd been expecting.

All the while during his scuffle with Bullock, Clint had heard gunshots going off on either side of him. He knew that the sheriff and Evans's men had been trading lead, but couldn't see much more than that. Now, he could make out two figures crouched behind what little cover the posts and barrels on the porch could provide. There were three of them and Evans was still huddled down among them.

Clint glanced over his shoulder to check on the sheriff. Williams was still on two feet, but he was clutching his side and blood was pouring steadily between his fingers.

"Sheriff, get down," Clint yelled.

But it was too late. Williams coughed once and took another shot with his pistol before falling onto his back with a loud thump.

Boots scraped along the porch and when Clint turned to see what was happening, he saw one of the hired guns leaning out from behind a post to take a shot.

The gunman was quick, but Clint was still quicker and two shots blasted through the air. Clint's landed first, hitting the gunman in the chest and spinning him like a wild top. That caused the gunman's shot to go wide and it punched a hole into the street.

That shooter's eyes were already glazed over as he landed beside the body of another gunman who must have been taken down by Sheriff Williams.

The only ones who remained were Evans and two of his men. Clint held his gun at the ready, still fighting through the painful throbbing that coursed through his skull. Having his senses impaired even in the slightest put Clint on his guard. His eyes darted between the remaining men, and his body was ready to react at the slightest provocation.

Suddenly, both of the gunmen looked at each other and shook their heads. One of them tossed his gun to the ground and lifted his hands in the air.

"What!?" Evans shouted. "What the hell are you doing? He's hurt! Can't you see that?"

But the gunman simply walked off the porch and laced his fingers behind his head.

Turning to look at the gunman who still had hold of his weapon, Evans sputtered in disbelief. He was too flustered to even get out a coherent word.

That last gunman turned to his employer and shrugged. "He's right, Mister Evans. This has gone too far and gotten too messy. Mister Lowry won't like it one bit."

"But I can talk to Lowry," Evans pleaded. "I can pay you double your salary and you can go wherever you want. Just finish this! That's an order!"

"I take orders from Mister Lowry," the gunman said simply. "And he's only gonna want one thing when he hears about this."

Before Evans could say another word, the gunman took aim and fired off a quick shot, which landed squarely in the fat man's heart, spilling blood all over his perfectly tailored suit. Before he could drop, Evans was hit again. He died with his eyes still gaping in shock at the man who he'd trusted with his life.

Clint had almost taken a shot at the gunman who'd fired, but even through the painful fog behind his eyes, he could tell that the gunman wasn't firing at him. When he saw who the target was, he kept his Colt on target just in case the shooter got any more ideas.

But once Evans was dead, the gunman pitched his weapon to the ground and lifted his hands in the air. He walked calmly over to his partner and waited.

Clint wasn't about to walk over to them just yet. "You two have any more guns on you?" he asked.

"Strapped to my leg in my left boot," one of them replied.

"There's a knife on my back, under my coat," said the other.

Watching both shooters like a hawk, Clint asked, "And I suppose you're just going to turn yourselves in? Even though you might hang if you go to jail."

The first gunman shook his head. "It's better than what Mister Lowry will do to us. After what happened here, he won't be none too happy and I don't want to wind up buried at that ranch. I seen what happened to men who let him down. And this . . . well, this will get him madder than he's ever been."

"What about you?" Clint asked the second man.

"I'm with him," he said, nodding toward his partner. "Lowry's got men that don't do nothin' but tear men up while they're still breathin'. I know. I seen it. Even a noose is better than that."

Although Clint's first reaction was to assume the killers were lying, he couldn't see the first trace of deception in their eyes. In fact, what he saw there was anger tainted with fear. If they were going to make a move, they would have done so already. But they were apparently too frightened of a man who wasn't even in this state.

All Clint could think at that moment was just what the hell kind of dirt a man like Peyton Lowry had beneath his fingernails. Then again, after taking another look at the two men in front of him, he decided he'd really rather not know.

At that moment, the door to the hotel creaked open and Elena peeked outside. "C-Clint?" she said in a meek voice. "Is it safe to come out now?"

Behind her, the man who'd worked the desk of the Hilltop Lodge was trying to get a better look at what was going on at his front step. Both of them gasped when they saw the bodies piled up outside and immediately ducked back inside.

Clint stepped forward, kicked away the guns that were laying on the ground and took the holdout weapons that both men had told him about. After searching them quickly, he found out that they were being completely honest with him and had no other weapons.

In fact, as some of Williams's deputies rushed over to take the gunmen into custody, Clint thought he detected a look of relief come onto the killers' faces.

FORTY-FOUR

"I feel like such an idiot," James Halliwell said for about the tenth time since Clint had gotten back.

After hearing what had happened at the lodge and how both Frye and Evans were now out of the picture, James shook his head and swore at himself again. "Jesus, I feel so damn stupid. All this time I was going on about driving some herd of cattle when that ranch was sitting on top of some rich man's dirty laundry."

Margaret Halliwell patted her son on the head lovingly. "I should've told you all about it, son. But I didn't want to pull you into something where you might get hurt." Looking down at the wounds she'd been tending, she shrugged and added, "Well . . . hurt anymore."

"It's not your fault," James replied.

"It's not anyone's fault," Clint spoke up. "This whole thing might have gone better if I would have understood what was going on a little sooner. Even now when I think about it, I feel more dizzy than when that side of beef knocked my brains loose." Although Clint's senses were back to normal, he still had a headache that raged inside him like a forest fire.

Mrs. Halliwell stood up and went to moisten the towel

she'd been using to dab at James's forehead. "Oh what a tangled web we weave, when we first try to deceive." Looking around at all the faces staring at her, she smirked and said, "Or something like that."

Clint smiled back at the old woman. "I'd say that about sums it up."

All this time, Elena had been sitting in the corner of the cottage, rocking her little brother on her lap. The youngest Halliwell child hadn't said a word since Clint and Elena had returned. When he thought about it, Clint couldn't remember that kid saying anything since he'd been there.

"Is he all right?" Clint asked.

Elena smiled and shook her head. "After all that's happened, you're worried about Eddie?" Patting the kid's stomach and squeezing him tightly, she said, "I think he'll be just fine."

The child looked up at Clint as though he was about to say something when a loud crash came from the other side of the room. Eddie and Clint both looked in that direction to find James rubbing his fist after slamming it against his bedside table.

"That ranch was supposed to give us a better life," he said. "Mister Adams was right when he said that Lowry wouldn't forget any of this."

Clint walked up to James's bed and handed him a cup of water. "There's not a lot you can do about that right now," he said. "Just relax and try to mend up. After all the dirt Evans kicked up, I'd say the last thing Lowry wants is to kick up any more. The papers that were here are gone and the papers at that ranch are gone, too."

"So you really had someone fetch those for you?"

"Fetch? No," Clint replied. "Burn? Yes. See for yourself."

Clint took out a folded piece of paper from his shirt

pocket and handed it to James. It was a telegram and it read:

"WENT TO RANCH AND LOOKED WHERE YOU TOLD
ME **STOP** FOUND SOME DOCUMENTS AND NOT MUCH
ELSE **STOP** BURNED THEM AND DON'T CARE WHAT
THEY WERE **STOP**"

"Who did this for you?" James asked after he was done reading.

"Someone I helped out a year or so ago when I passed through Nebraska. After what those gunmen said, I'd wager there's plenty more at that ranch besides some papers, but losing those should be enough to rattle Lowry a bit. He'll be too busy digging everything else up and moving it to worry about you.

"Just do yourself a favor and don't tell anyone else about this or you might stumble into another one of those tangled webs your mother was talking about. And you might want to move away sometime soon. You know . . . get that fresh start you wanted."

Once again, James's face clouded over. "Move away with what?"

Clint dug into his jacket pocket and pulled out a wad of bills. "This should get you started."

"No, no," James said while shaking his head. "I can't accept that. Not after everything you've done for us."

Clint held the money out in the palm of his hand. "It'll make me feel better. I can't just leave you all here without knowing that you'll be able to make ends meet. Besides, I won it in a poker game and like they say, easy come . . ."

Elena reached out and took the money from Clint's hand and said, ". . . easy go. My brother may be too proud to take this, but I'm not. Thank you so much, Clint. For everything."

Tipping his hat, Clint bid his farewells and headed out the front door. Elena left with him.

When they got outside, Clint stopped and faced Elena. "You went over the line back there," he said.

She put on her best innocent expression. "Just following orders."

"I asked you to spread the word that I'd left, not go screaming into the viper's den."

"Is there anything I can do to make it up to you?" Elena asked while slipping her hands around his neck.

"You know . . . I just might be able to come up with something."

FORTY-FIVE

Clint's hotel room was nothing different than any of the other rooms he'd rented all across the country. There was a bed and not much else, which was just fine by him. After all, a bed was the only thing Elena had been interested in when she'd followed him back into town.

Knowing that he was set to leave and that she might not see him again for any number of years, they locked themselves in the no-frills room and Elena peeled the dress down off her shoulders. By the time she'd walked over to the bed, the only thing she wore was her ankle-high boots and a wide, excited smile.

"I thought you'd had your fill of excitement today," Clint said as he placed his hands upon her full, rounded hips.

"I was scared to death out there," she said. "And now I'm just happy to be alive. So happy that I want to celebrate . . . with you."

With the blood still heated in Clint's veins after all that had happened, he felt an extra pulse of energy flow through him when Elena pressed her naked body up against his own. The adrenaline built to an even higher level as she worked him out of his shirt and pants before pushing him back onto the bed.

Elena climbed on top of him, straddling Clint's hips while grinding herself against his growing erection. All the while, Clint ran his hands over her back and pulled her down so that he could run his tongue between her breasts.

The taste of her skin was especially sweet and Clint couldn't stop kissing Elena's body. His lips brushed against her nipples and then he took the rigid pink nubs into his mouth one at a time.

Elena groaned with delight and shifted her hips so that she could lower herself down onto Clint's rigid cock. At the moment of penetration, both of them had to catch their breath. Elena settled all the way down until he was fully inside of her, clenching her eyes tightly shut as a little orgasm rippled through her body.

Once again, Clint's heart was racing. Only this time, it wasn't because of the bullets flying through the air around his head. Now, he found himself at the opposite end of the spectrum, savoring life to its fullest by indulging in one of the finest things it had to offer.

Thinking along those lines, Clint took in the sight of Elena's smoothly contoured body as she began to slowly ride on top of him. Her full breasts swayed and her hair fell over her shoulders as she picked up her pace and threw herself completely into the moment.

Clint reached around to hold her round buttocks, letting his body move wherever his desire wished to go. His hands wandered along her back and guided Elena's steady bouncing. His hips shifted back and forth, occasionally pumping upward, which caused Elena to moan louder.

For that moment, there was no longer anything else in Clint's world except for that little room and the beautiful woman on top of him. Their bodies moved perfectly together and just when he thought he knew what she was going to do, Clint was surprised by Elena.

Her hands touched him in all the right spots and she knew just when to clench her muscles around him.

All the pain in Clint's body went away, replaced by the building flood of pleasure that was quickly approaching its summit.

Neither one of them wanted to hold off any longer. The sensations were too intense and the pleasure was too great.

Elena arched her back and slid her fingers through her hair, giving Clint a glorious view of her proud breasts and hard nipples. Her stomach heaved and her muscles strained as a second orgasm caused her to cry out loud.

Clint grabbed hold of her firm backside and pumped up between her legs, his own climax coming as he pounded deeply inside of her.

FORTY-SIX

When they were both spent, Elena collapsed onto the bed. Clint lay right where he was, unable to move even if he'd wanted to.

And just when he thought he'd truly forgotten about the rest of the world, the rest of the world came back to knock on Clint's door.

"What was that?" Elena asked.

Clint let out a tired breath. "Someone's knocking. Just ignore it."

They both fell quiet, but the knocking went on . . . and on . . . and on.

Muttering under his breath, Clint threw on some clothes and got up to answer the door. When he pulled it open, he glared into the eyes of a small, meek-looking man wearing a brown tweed suit. The expression on Clint's face was grim enough to freeze the little man with his hand in mid-air.

"What. Do. You. Want?" Clint growled.

The little man glanced nervously at Clint and then tried to get a look past him. "Uh, excuse the intrusion, but is Elena Halliwell in that room?"

Clint started to get a nervous feeling in the pit of his

stomach. Whoever this man was, though, he already seemed to know his facts. "Yes," he said. "She's here."

"Then that would make you Clint Adams."

"Yeah. Who are you?"

When the little man smiled, it seemed to be more of a formality than a true expression of emotion. "You don't know me personally, but I represent the interests of Mister Kyle Bagley."

"Look, this matter is over," Clint started to say, but he was cut off by the little man's insistent voice. "I know, I know. Mister Bagley heard about what happened here and what you've done to Mister Lowry's representatives as well as the materials that were rather creatively misplaced. He's . . . quite pleased."

"How does he know about all of this?"

"He has his sources, Mister Adams. He keeps a close eye on things that involve Mister Lowry since he is my employer's largest competitor. I'm only here to express his gratitude for what you did to stifle Mister Lowry's enterprise."

Clint watched every move the little man made, scanning the hallway for any sign of trouble. "I'm sure I didn't do much except—"

"No need to be modest. Anyway . . . I can tell you're busy and so I'll ask that you give this to Miss Halliwell." The little man slid his hand beneath his coat and before he could do anything else, Clint's hand was pressed against his throat.

"If I see a gun come out of there," Clint said, "I'll have to make you regret it."

His face turning bright red, the little man gasped a few times before sputtering, "N-no gun. H-here. Take it."

Slowly, the little man's hand came out of his jacket. Rather than any kind of weapon, he was holding a fat envelope wrapped with twine around its middle.

Clint took the envelope and used his thumb to open it

just wide enough to get a look inside. When he saw the contents, he let go of the little man's throat. "Sorry about that," he said.

"Not at all," the little man said while rubbing at his reddened neck. "Under the circumstances, I quite understand."

Inside the envelope, there was enough money to choke a horse. Most of the bills were twenties with a couple fifties mixed in. Clint estimated there to be at least a couple thousand dollars in there.

"Was anyone on Bagley's payroll?" Clint asked.

"No, sir. This is merely a thank you from my employer. Tell the Halliwells to enjoy it in good health." With that, the little man turned around and walked away.

"What was that all about?" Elena asked when Clint shut the door and came back to the bed.

Tossing the envelope onto the bed, Clint said, "It looks like someone noticed the hurt we put on Lowry's men and liked what they saw."

"Good lord," Elena said after thumbing through the money. "Do we get to keep this?"

"Your mother's fond of old sayings, so here's one for you: Don't look a gift horse in the mouth. Take the money and use it to start fresh somewhere far from that house of yours."

"And far from Nebraska," she added.

Clint laughed and shook his head. "One thing's for sure . . . I'll want my poker money back."

Elena smiled and dug the money from her dress, which was piled up on the floor. Reclining on the bed, she fanned out Clint's money and spread it all over her naked body. "If you want it . . . come and get it."

After dealing with the Halliwells and their problems this long, Clint knew better than to bother himself with trying to straighten any of it out. He knew he didn't have a prayer of figuring all of the angles. Some webs were just going to stay tangled no matter how hard he pulled at their edges.

So rather than work on another headache, he lowered himself onto Elena and started plucking his money off of her with his teeth.

Watch for

A DAY IN THE SUN

254th novel in the exciting GUNSMITH series
from Jove

Coming in February!